FINDING NATHAN

The Jordan Spagnato Series

Book Two

H.J. Harley

Contains adult language.

Fiction. Romance. Suspense.

Cover and book design by eBook Prep www.ebookprep.com

First Edition, May, 2014
ISBN: 978-1-61417-544-5

ePublishing Works!
www.epublishingworks.com

DEDICATION

Travis, thank you for always dealing with my shit and my love for RP. I promise you if Kate Beckinsale comes looking for you I'll be cheering you on. :P I love you.

ACKNOWLEDGEMENTS

This would have never happened without these great peeps…

Kristin-Phillips-Delcambre "They did what was best for Old Yeller. I promise you."

Dawn and her Bush…G.W. that is.

Jenni, once again you were there for me and my needy self. <3

Lisa, thank you so much for your input. Smack that ass!

To the man at Starbucks that insisted the chair I sat in everyday was his, you can have it back now.

Amy, I still can't believe we pulled it off.

Finally, to 'The Unicorns', you guys are the best. Here's to always 'Moving Forward'

CHAPTER 1

Going to the DMV was never on my list of top ten favorite things to do. Going to the DMV sleep deprived, cranky, and smelling like spit up made it that much *more* pleasurable.

"Harper? Jordan Marie Harper?"

I vaguely heard my name through my dream-like state, and sat straight up in what may have been the most uncomfortable chair my ass had ever been in.

"Jordie?" Rachel nudged me. "Wake up and go get your shit. Give me Nate."

She reached over and took my little man from my arms.

I wiped the drool off my face as I walked up to the counter to get the first glimpse of my new mug shot. I felt like complete ass. It had been a long ten years between kids and I'd forgotten just how demanding they were. I loved my kids and I'd have done anything for them, but some sleep would've been glorious.

I shuffled my feet back to the entrance where Rachel was waiting. She was just as ready to get the hell out of there as I was. She snatched the license out of my hand to admire the new credentials.

"Oh. My. Gawd, you look like Nate Harper's Zombie Bride," she snorted.

"Eff off," I quipped with no effort and a small smile as we walked out to my truck. "I need some sleep, Rach. He's up all night," I whined as I took Nate from her and secured him in his car seat.

"I hath no pity on thee. You're the one who refuses the help. Seriously, it's like Nathan isn't *allowed* to be a father at times." She reached for her seatbelt as I started the truck.

"Rachel, he works all day, sometimes all day and half the night. I can't ask him to stay up all night with him."

"You aren't asking him. He volunteers. You just take away his man card and tell him no." She rolled her eyes as I pulled out of the parking lot. "When will you learn you can't and don't have to do this alone? You're married. Say it with me, mar-ried. M-A-R-R-I-E-D now. Comprende?"

"Exactly, and I'm trying to be the best wife possible. There are a million chicks who wish they could be me and I don't want to give him a reason to replace me." My voice cracked a bit.

"Yeah, okay, you hormonal nightmare. Like Nathan sees any other woman than you? Please, you're a dumbass for even saying that. You *know* how much he loves you," she said as she put on a fresh coat of lip gloss.

Just as we pulled up to my place, Nathan Jr. fell asleep. I was so thankful because if he was napping that meant I could take an almost three-hour nap before Emma got home from school. I hugged Rachel goodbye before she headed out and the phone rang as I walked to the front of the bar. I put Nate down in his car seat carrier to answer it. I could see it was Nathan on the caller ID.

"Hey, babe," I huffed. *Damn heifer, you're out of shape.*

"Jordan? Is everything okay? Where are you?" He sounded agitated.

"I had to get my license renewed. It's a *wonderful* pic–" I began to say but he cut me off.

"Jesus, Jordie, I guess you forgot that we were meeting Gabby today, at ten a.m.?"

"Oh crap. That was today?" I forgot we had an appointment with the realtor. How could I forget something like that? Especially since my apart– *our* apartment had turned into a sardine can overnight. Nathan didn't have a ton of stuff but between what he'd moved in, then add the baby and all his new stuff, it felt like ten pounds of shit crammed into a five pound bag in there.

As if that weren't reason enough, things were getting a bit ridiculous how the paparazzi had set up shop on the curb out front. Then there were the deliveries on a daily basis. I understood how grateful Nathan was for his fans but it had gotten out of control. Without Isobel and Todd giving the paps info, it'd become a free for all. It got so bad that Frank had to move in downstairs, which I didn't mind at all.

There were many reasons to move but only one to stay. My bar. It wasn't much but it was mine. Yeah, Nathan had money and I became his wife but that doesn't make it mine, well, it made it mine by default but not definition. Whereas the bar was mine, business was great and I saw no reason to sell it. Compromising, we decided on the Upper East Side of Manhattan to allow me to be close to the bar plus security was tighter which would give Frank a bit of a break. Emma's routine wouldn't change much, and

Central Park was within walking distance. All right, there were a ton of positives in moving there. I was just thankful Nathan compromised so well.

"I'll be home in twenty. Do you need anything?" His tone had evened out. Okay, so I was also thankful for Nathan's ability to let things go quickly.

"Bagel. I would love an everything bagel with cream cheese, and a large coffee light and sweet, please." I could hear the weariness in my voice. I had no energy left to spare but I didn't want it to be obvious.

"Uh, babe. How about you lay off the carbs and caf–"

"What? I just had a baby. My ass isn't going to snap back into shape right away and an effin' bagel with some cream cheese isn't going to make me gain ten pounds. I'll run it off at the gym later. Jesus. Ya' know, never mind. No bagel." I snapped this out in one quick sentence before he could finish his.

He gave a chuckle. "So. Like I was saying, why don't you cut back on the carbs and caffeine so you can get some sleep when I get home? Mom and Dad are closing on their brownstone Tuesday and they flew in last night. Going to take Nate to spend some time with G Ma and G Pa. Plus we have the MET thing tonight. She can watch the kids, and FYI your ass looks great." His voice was just dripping with humor. "So sensitive. I love you. Be home in twenty."

"I love you, too. Sorry," I whispered. My shoulders slumped and I hung my head, embarrassed by the snap assumption I made about what he was going to say.

"Stop, its fine. See ya' in a few," he said, before cutting the call.

I looked at the receiver and smiled. *Welp, at least he still loves me.*

Just then my text alert went off. I pulled my cell from my pocket quickly, hoping it wouldn't wake Nate up.

I love you and our kids more than anything...and your ass. I love your ass. One carb and caffeine filled bfast headed your way XO

I smiled. He always knew how to make me do that, no matter what my mood was. Which I'll admit, had been all over the place since I had the baby. My hormones were so out of whack. Nathan had regained his memory about three weeks before Nate was born, so everything changed at lightning speed once again. After spending seven months without him, pregnant and hormonal, I had to readjust to him being there again. An adjustment I was more than happy to make. I was whole again. Not that I fell apart at the seams while Nathan was—um, what should I call it—recovering? Yeah, while he was recovering I was okay. I didn't lock myself in a room wasting away in my own filth and crying for months on end, or anything like that. Life went on. It was just at a slower pace. Partly because my heart was so heavy, but mainly because I was pregnant as hell and I couldn't move any faster.

When he walked in twenty-three minutes later I handed Nate over, kissed them both then as I picked up my bagel and coffee to head upstairs.

"I love you but I'm so tired. Wake me up when Emma gets home please," I said as I dragged my tired body upstairs dodging a pile of laundry, a baby swing and two huge boxes of diapers. I was like the luckiest woman in the world.

I'd slept most of the afternoon away. Nathan woke me up around five thirty pm because he had that charity event at the MET. I was supposed to go with him but in the end I wasn't up to it. He took Emma. I thought for sure he'd take his mom, so that was an unexpected treat for the kid. When I finally made it downstairs, their attire for the evening had just arrived along with the 'Esteem Team.' Jean-Philippe, who cringed every time I called him JP, was Nathan's French native stylist. Brantley was Jean Phillip's assistant, and Naomi took care of hair and makeup. The three of them together were like watching a very fashionable train wreck. Naomi was hilarious. She'd always throw herself right in the middle of JP and Brantley's tiffs. Like her southern belle twang was the voice of reason amongst the two slapping each other as if they had T-Rex arms.

"Well, well, well, aren't you looking fabulous this evening, little lady?" JP bent and kissed Emma on both cheeks then stepped back to get a look at her. After he eyed her up and down, he clapped his hands together with a smile then snapped his fingers over his shoulder.

"The emerald one, Brantley. Definitely the emerald Versace for this little gem."

I was close enough by that time to have heard Brantley mumble something along the lines of giving him an emerald foot in the ass. When I laughed, he looked up seemingly surprised I made out what he said, gave me a grin, and rolled his eyes.

"Nathan, take the maroon Gucci, try that on first with the black tie and let me see how it looks. I brought two in case you changed your mind," JP said as he dug through a clear storage box labeled 'Accessories.'

"In case *I* changed my mind, Jean Philippe?" Nathan chuckled.

JP pivoted around holding a black chiffon scarf up

in his hand. His smoky grey eyes flickered with humor. "Oh honey, don't I know you'd be perfectly happy going in that." He made a mock disgusted face as he flicked his wrist up and down, the scarf waving along with it, while he pointed out the jeans and T-shirt Nathan was wearing. "Now, please, go change. I don't have time to play cat and mouse with you tonight. I have this gorgeous girl to tend to."

JP picked up a pair of too high-heeled silver shoes, and walked over to Emma.

"Hey, JP, no on those shoes. She's ten and I don't need her breaking any bones."

I took the shoes from his hand and grabbed a different pair of silver shoes, with a shorter, chunkier heel. "There you go."

I kissed my daughter on the top of her head and went to sit at the dining room table where Naomi was setting up her station.

I liked talking to Naomi. She always had some sort of celebrity gossip to dish out to me. I admit it, I'd become a frequenter of the internet and tabloid sites the last few months. Some of the things they said about us would crack me up. Then again, some of the things they said about us made me want to go out front and high five them, in the face, with a park bench. It was ridiculous. There was this one picture plastered all over the covers of these rag mags and internet sites. It was of me, Nathan and Emma. I was in mid sneeze while Nathan grabbed Emma by the arm to pull her out of the way of a bike delivery guy none of us had seen speeding towards us until the last second. That picture was passed around and made out to be that Nathan had hit me and went after Emma next. These jackholes totally photoshopped the bike guy out of the picture, so pathetic. It was those days that I missed Isobel and Todd even more than average.

"So, whatcha' got for me?" I plopped in the chair and propped my head up with my hands, looking at Naomi in interest.

"Girl, you don't even want to know." She scoffed as she checked over her scissors.

"Oh, I do I do though. C'mon." I leaned forward wide-eyed with anticipation.

"All right, you gossip queen. Calm down." She laughed and took a seat. "Okay, don't tell Nathan I told you this because he will just say I'm causing drama, but you'll read about it somewhere eventually." She went back to setting up her workstation.

"I won't," I said. I couldn't hide the fact that my curiosity level piqued through the roof. "Out with it already."

"So, I was on Twitter after that horrid pic of Nathan supposedly beating you guys up on the street went viral. People were going on and on about it, and it started trending. I was reading the tweets and I came across these really crazy ones. Some were all about bashing Nathan and others were defending him and you. Then I noticed this one chick was talking about a forum. I followed that link to some online shrine to Nate. You have got to see this place. Talk about fifty shades of cray cray." She placed the last of her equipment on the table and turned to face me. "I'm not even playin'. These bitches have lost their damn mind. Some of the shit they say is so out there. They ship Nate and Lena hardcore, and this other chick. I forget her name…"

I interrupted her. "Wait, what? They ship them? Ship them where?" I was lost.

"Not actually shipping them somewhere. They 'ship them, like as in relation*ship*. It's the term that's used.

Shipping. Strange but whatevs. Anyhow, some of the posts on there were just ridiculous. Some have a theory that you and Nathan, and the whole dead ex-husband thing, was something put together by a studio to boost Nate's image and your bar's popularity. Then take this whole magic love story and turn it into hell in a cell for you guys."

"What? Why would they want to do that?" The words came out a bit strained because my mouth was so dry from sitting there with it open throughout our conversation. Mouth breather problems.

"Why? Well, let's take a stab at this. For Nate's next block buster, to keep him in the spotlight, to make him out to be a hero. Because it's Hollywood and they're not happy until the life has been sucked from every situation they could possibly make a dime off of? That's why." She laughed and stood up as she finished her sentence.

Nathan put his hands on my shoulders and massaged them lightly. I looked up at him, resting the back of my head against his stomach.

"What are you two gossip mongers going on about over here?" He bent over and kissed my forehead before I looked back over at Naomi.

"Girl talk, bucko. Nothing else. Now have a seat. You need a trim before I start on Emma." She winked at me as she patted the chair for Nathan to sit down.

CHAPTER 2

After I fed Nate, I took him downstairs to Nathan's mom. She had come over to spend some time with the baby. Plus, I was pretty sure she knew I was a chicken shit when it came to staying home alone. I guess subconsciously I still wasn't over what happened with Jason and all that mess. When I got downstairs, she was folding the towels.

"Mom, you don't have to do that. I'll get it. Here, take the baby. He wants his G Ma." I smiled and stood next to her.

After Nathan and I got married, I once made the mistake of calling his mother by her first name, Fiona. She hugged me and said, "None of that Jordie, I'm Mom now." I just stood there frozen with my arms at my side, stiff as a shot of Wild Turkey. I thought about how long it had been since I'd last said that word. When I snapped out of it a few seconds later, I hugged her back. "All right...Mom." It must've been obvious I was trying the word on for size, because Fiona laughed, drew back, and took my face in her hands. "Well, that was convincing." She kissed my forehead. "You'll adjust."

By now, I was used to calling her Mom.

"Oh hush your face. You know I don't mind. You have so much going on here. This is the least I can do to help out." She said the last half of the sentence in a baby talk voice as she took Nate out of my arms and smiled at her grandson.

"Thank you, I appreciate it." I gave her a kiss on the cheek. "Now, mind if I steal two of these and hop in the shower?"

I picked up two unfolded towels and was careful not to say the words 'real quick'. I wanted this shower to last. I was practically salivating at the thought of an over three minute hot shower.

I turned the water on full blast, hot as I could take it, threw my clothes in a rumpled pile on the floor, and got in. I washed up quick, shaved my legs, then I stood there and savored every last drop of the steamy goodness as it washed over me. It wasn't until I was drying my hair a little while later that something Naomi had said to me earlier popped in my head. *What did she call it again? Shopping? Shipping. Yes, shipping.* I had to look into this.

'Shipping' according to Urban Dictionary dot com is a term used to describe fan fictions that take previously created characters and put them as a pair. Or it can be two real celebrities that are being shipped. It usually refers to romantic relationships, but it can refer to platonic ones as well. Just think of 'shipping' as short for 'relationship'. It generally uses the initials of the characters shipped or a combination of the names, though this is not a rule.

So, people were shipping Nathan with someone else? That raised an eyebrow on me. I needed to know all about this shipping business. I ran downstairs to see how Mom and Nate were doing, and grabbed a drink. I knew I'd be up there a while. She was on the couch with him out cold in his pack-n-play. She was watching something on her iPad.

"What are you watching?" I popped over her shoulder.

"Oh, the online coverage of the MET event."

The Metropolitan Museum of Art was one of Emma's favorite places. Having the experience of being there for that event, most likely would change it to her favorite place.

"Did they walk yet?" I hovered behind her.

"Not yet. Come. Sit. Relax," she said in a worried, motherly tone. "Do you want me to fix you something to eat? You're looking pale, Jordan."

"Ma, I'm fine. Thank you, though. I got my green tea. All is right with the world." I plopped down next to her and sat Indian style while we watched the red carpet event together.

After a few more couples, I caught sight of Nathan and Emma a few feet back posing for pictures. Emma fidgeted a bit and blinked a lot. My guess was the camera flashes were bothering her eyes. The girl who was being interviewed at that moment was new to Hollywood according to the host. Her name was Bristol Santana. When the hostess asked who she was looking forward to working with in the future, she tossed her long dark hair and jacked her thumb over her shoulder, glancing in Nathan's direction.

"I can't wait to work with Nate Harper."

Her smile was so big you could barely see her blue eyes. The host said something that I didn't really pay much attention to after seeing her enthusiasm to work with my husband. As the up-and-comer walked off, Frank ushered Nathan and Emma towards their spot in front of the camera. There they stood, my beautiful daughter and gorgeous husband. Above the noise of the screaming fans, a woman's voice could be heard. "I love you, Nate!" she screeched and I nearly fell off the couch when Emma rolled her eyes on live television.

I busted out laughing along with Fiona. Frank cracked a stifled grin as well.

Since Nathan was standing next to her, he was none the wiser to her reaction. Emma just smiled sweetly at the interviewer as she asked Nathan questions.

When they were finished and headed inside the venue Fiona said, "Well if she isn't her mother's daughter." She chuckled and got up off the couch.

"What can I say? She's got her mamma's back." I grabbed my tea off the table and gave her a hug. "Thank you, Ma, I really appreciate you helping me out."

"Oh please, you act as if this is a chore and I'm some selfless martyr." She chuckled again. "Believe me, I'm being selfish. I love spending time with my grandchildren, Jordie."

She winked at me before she picked up a still sleeping Nate. I gave him a gentle rub on the top of his head and smiled.

"Whatever your reasons, thank you." I kissed her on the cheek and headed towards the stairs. Since I had the night off courtesy of my mother-in-law, I took full advantage.

Once I was back upstairs, I plopped on our bed and opened up my laptop. I typed in 'Nate Harper shipping.' I know–lame, but it was a start. There was a ton of links listed for free shipping of various items with Nathan's face plastered on them. I laughed at the fuzzy slippers but the underwear that had 'Mrs. Harper' across the ass, along with the pillowcases, completely creeped me out. I clicked on the underwear link.

"One-thousand in stock? How much are these mofos? I'll buy them all. What. The. Fuck. I'm Mrs. Harper."

I felt my face getting hot. I mean, okay, I *knew* women, all kinds of women, hundreds of thousands of women of all ages 'loved' Nate Harper. I got that a long time ago. I was fine with it because I knew Nathan loved me. Not only me but our family. We were an actual family. When he walked through the doors, he was no longer Nate. He was Nathan or Daddy. I thought back to the night I attempted to give him a nickname. I felt like a nagging mother having to say 'Nathan this or Nathan that, Nathan, Nathan, Nathan'. The obvious nickname Nate was taken by the outside world. I needed something of my own and nut-job wasn't cutting it, especially in public.

"I need a nick name for you. I'm so over having to say Nathan all the time when everyone else gets to call you Nate." I said to him as he put his hand on my stomach and traced a few of my ten-week-old stretch marks with his finger.

"Really? You didn't mind it so much five minutes ago when you were screaming it." He laughed as I swatted his hand and shrieked at him.

"Oh my God, you so did not just say that!?" I caught him in the face with a pillow and he flipped over on top of me in a flash, wedged himself between my legs and propped himself up on his elbows.

"You love it." He grinned.

"Oh, and you don't, Mister Clench-my-teeth and growl?" I started to laugh harder when he buried his head between my neck and shoulder then took a playful bite while he growled.

"That's it, that'll be my nick name for you." I slapped his back in excitement as he lifted his head and gave me a confused look.

"Mister Clench-my-teeth and growl?" He snickered playfully.

I laughed even harder when he repeated it and I responded, "Sure, why not?"

"I like that you call me Nathan. It's a clear distinction between the two. Just like you said, out there, Nate…in here." He buried his face between my breasts. "I'm just Nathan."

"In my tits, you're just Nathan?" I tugged on his messier than normal hair with a smile that hurt my face.

"No, in here." He traced his finger over my heart. "In the only place it matters. You, Emma and Nate. Our family. So you see, I quite like being Nathan."

It was then I realized that it didn't matter what I called him, as long as I called him. He loved me, and the kids. I mean for Christ sakes he loved us so much it forced his brain past amnesia. I finished up the last of my jealousy rant and started the search for 'Nate Harper relationship.' Well, that just opened a can of cray-cray like none other. I hoped I was ready for this because if not we'd be in need of some serious couples therapy by the looks of some of these results. I don't know why but I hit the image tab. Bad idea. My jaw was where my stomach should've been and my stomach was on the floor. Holy shit. There was picture after picture of Nathan with me, and other women. Some were the tabloid covers from when we were apart but most of them weren't. As I scrolled down I began to notice pictures that were of me and Nathan but it wasn't my face. There was a different head on my body.

"What the…what is this?" I said out loud as I shook my head in disbelief. I clicked back to the web tab and checked out some of the results. The weird pictures would have to wait until I had the brain capacity to deal with that mess.

There were just a few articles about him but when I scrolled down a little more, there was a link to 'Nate-Nation: Everything Nate Harper'. I clicked on it and began browsing through the limited threads I could see being non-registered and all. One caught my eye instantly. 'Nordie is a Fraud' it read in bold letters with 10,348 replies. First of all, WTF is a Nordie? And who is comes up with this shit?" I questioned out loud, to myself. I scrolled down and saw the answer. "So, its names mashed together like Bennifer, or Brangelina? Too much time on your hands people. Too. Much. Time." I should've never opened the Internet can of worms with post-partum hormones still coursing through me because holy shit, I was a hot mess. I couldn't wrap my head around the fact that for every one person slinging the poo, there were twenty others picking it up and believe it. Really? People really thought we had a fake relationship? Fans 'shipped' him with the 'up-and-coming' Bristol Santana? Some even said the whole thing with Jason coming back was staged for publicity, and once mine and Nate's 'contract was up', he'd be free to do whomever he wanted and be happy. Which led to a whole new level of 'Waits, WTF's and Are you kiddings' because all it did was bring up more questions for me. People didn't like me? Why? Nathan wasn't happy? He looked miserable? I never noticed him looking miserable. Why would they want him with her? Or not believe we were married?

By the time Nathan and Emma got in, it was nearly eleven and my blood pressure was through the roof. Nathan's mom had tried to calm me down but the things I'd seen had my mind racing out of control. I was an absolute train wreck. I was upstairs when they came through the door but I could hear him talking to his mother, asking what was up with me. But after that it became hushed chatter. After a few moments of that, his mom suggested Emma go get ready for bed and say she'd check to see if I was still awake to say g'nite.

"But, I can hear her pacing upstairs. She isn't asleep," Emma said.

"Oh, well, I guess that answers that question. Go ahead, sweetie. Go get ready for bed, then go say goodnight." I heard Fiona loud and clear that time. Maybe that was her way of telling me to get my shit together because my kid shouldn't see me like this. I quickly closed up my laptop, grabbed my Kindle, and lay down on the bed.

Keep it together, it's not like he wrote any of that shit. Don't get all weepy and whiney on him. Keep the hormones in check and be cool.

When Nathan entered the bedroom, he was taking off his tie. He looked tired. He hung it over the doorknob and started to toe off his shoes.

"Hey, baby," he said after the second shoe was off, and began to walk over to the bed.

"Hey, handsome." I peered at him over the blank screen of my Kindle and then closed the cover. "How'd it go? Emma have a good time?"

"She had a blast. More interested in the exhibits than the event. Is everything okay with you?" He sat on the edge of the bed and laid back, exhaling loudly.

"Yep, everything's fine," I lied with a thin smile.

My stomach was in knots. I still couldn't believe those women called themselves fans. I was sure if Nathan knew about any of that, he wouldn't be too happy so I decided to keep it to myself. For the moment.

"You sure? Mom said you were a little...," he

paused and took my Kindle from my hands. "Upset."

*Why would she tell him that? Ugh...*I didn't want to explain this crap to him, not right then anyhow. He lay on his side and propped his head up on his hand.

"Look, I know some of the stuff people say online is nuts. You can't let it bother you. What made you go on an internet adventure anyhow? You don't normally do things like that. What's up?"

"Oh, it's nothing. I was just curious about something, and what do you mean some of the stuff people say is nuts? You mean you *know* about the crazy shit they say. Really?"

"Of course I know, Jordan. It's nothing new. Although, I'll admit since you and I got together it's escalated to somewhat alarming." He began unbuttoning his shirt.

"Alarming?" I sat up straight against the headboard. I've had enough alarming for one lifetime, I didn't want any more. I couldn't handle any more truthfully.

"Alarming in a 'Damn, where's their sense of sanity' sort of way, not as in 'crazy terrorist husband on the loose' way." He winked and stood up and finished undressing.

I swore to god, I had the hottest man on the planet.

Focus, horn dog.

Why was it that, anytime danger came up, I wanted to jump on him?

"I don't like it, Nathan. Some of those women were saying horrible things about you and me. About how I'm a terrible person and how bitchy I am. Like, when have I ever been bitchy other than at the hospital the night you got shot? And I wasn't even bitchy to your fans, I just lost my shit on the press. Oh, and did you know *that* wasn't even real? That was all a set up by your people for publicity for the movie you were working on. And don't forget the contract we're in.

What the fuck? A contract? Really, Nathan?" I threw my hands up and dropped them with a slap on my thighs.

He tied the string on his shorts with a quick laugh. "Oh, that's my personal favorite. The 'contract.'"

"You really know *all* about this stuff? You know how they put someone else's head on my body in pictures, and how you look miserable when you're with me. Are you miserable, Nathan?" My voice squeaked out two octaves too high and he gave me that lopsided grin he knew drove me mad, pulled me out of the bed and drew me in close to him.

"Do I *feel* miserable, Jordan?" He nudged his hip against me lightly and I could feel him.

"I'm serious, Nathan. All of that…" I nodded my head back towards my laptop, "was a huge mind fuck and not just because I'm emotional or any hormone shit. *Any woman* would feel the same, if they were talking about their husband that way."

I put my forehead on his chest and sobbed. All right, maybe I was a little emotional…okay fine, I was a hot mess. But who could blame me? Some of those chicks were down right vicious.

"This one chick on the 'Nate-Nation' boards keeps referring to me as 'ratchet.' What the fuck is ratchet? A tool? Why does she hate me so much?" I looked up at him all bleary eyed.

"Heh, so you found Nate-Nation?" He rolled his eyes and smiled. "I'm not a fan of that site at all. Of all the sites, it figures you'd find that one. I wish you hadn't. It's all very catty and full of delusions of grandeur. And you are most definitely not 'ratchet.'" He nudged me again and gave me that crooked grin that I couldn't resist.

I did find that one though. Delusional or not, I saw what they were saying. Why did these women think they knew my husband?

"Look at me." He tilted my chin up. "You are the strongest woman I've ever known and you have some pretty thick skin. Something triggered this. What's going on in there?" He tapped my forehead lightly.

I sighed and rested my head on his chest so he wouldn't see the tears forming.

Just drop it, Jordan. You can't change it and he can't control what others say. This isn't his fault. Handle it, and yourself.

"You're right. It was stupid of me to go down that rabbit hole. I knew what to expect. I guess my curiosity got the best of me. I'm over it." I gave him a small smile in hopes of convincing him. *And myself.*

CHAPTER 3

The smooth elevator ride and nearly angelic ding that followed as we reached the 33rd floor reminded me of where we were—on the West Side of Manhattan, Trump Place, Riverside Drive. *On the West Side.* Of course, there were plenty of apartments and penthouses available on the East Side, but there was no way on God's green earth we were spending that sort of money on a place smaller than mine.

We'd gone back and forth about that for a few days. I couldn't wrap my head around spending 2.7 mil for a thousand square foot apartment. Although, I have to admit the thought of not having that little E. in my address bugged me. A lot. I loved the East Village. Period. It'd always been the down to earth, fun and trendy side of the island. Once you crossed over 42nd Street it was all suits and ties, business and Berkins. I *so* didn't want a Berkin. The reality of it was though, I could afford a Berkin. My life had changed so drastically from the previous year I pretty much had to live in a swank tank like this.

Nathan put his hand on the small of my back for me to get out of the elevator first. My reflection greeted me in the smoky colored, mirrored hallway. There were two apartments on the floor. Our Real Estate agent Gabby, turned to the left and the annoying as hell clickity-clack of her high heels led the way. Rachel's heels never sounded like that. Then again, Rachel never walked on Italian marble in an empty hallway...well, maybe she did when she went to Rome, but that didn't count. I didn't hear it. Once I walked past noisy heel girl, I tuned back into what she was saying about this nearly four thousand square foot penthouse monstrosity at 10.4 mil.

"I thought the point of haulin' our cookies over to the West Side was for a better value? At double the price of the East Side, I think we made a wrong turn somewhere," I snickered as she opened the door and flashed us a fabulous smile.

"Well, you actually are getting quite the value. This has more square footage and is a bit less per square foot."

The only thing though, either ol' Gabster didn't count on me looking to my left in the hallway mirror just as I entered, or she was too dumb to realize I could. I caught her rolling her eyes. When it finally dawned on the stupid twat that I saw her, she started fluttering her eyes like she was having a seizure or something, saying some dust flew into her eye when she opened the door.

"Yeah, the dust must be a real bitch in this sterile, non-windowed environment. I could understand how that happened." I flashed one of my sarcastic smirks at her.

She showed us around with her over-the-top, pretty words, and pleasant hand gestures. I can't even tell you how big this chick's balls had to have been to openly flirt with Nathan. I was so used to it that by then it didn't normally bother me, but today it made me twitchy. The view was amazing, and we would be the only ones with access to the rooftop terrace. That's how most of them were on the East Side; this was the only one we'd found on the West, which I loved for obvious reasons. Because not having a private rooftop would definitely suck, but also because Nate could never get up there. I loved being able to just go up there and read, or have a lazy night with Nathan in the hammock thingy he put up. By the time we hit the 'en-suite', you know, the room also known as a fucking bathroom, I'd had enough of it all.

"Okay, thank you. I've seen enough. Nathan, can we go please? Like, now." I turned on my heel and headed to the front of the apartment through the kitchen.

Jeeeesus, that was gorgeous. I swiped another real estate agent's card off the counter and headed out to the hallway. Nathan was a good distance behind me, but I heard him tell Gabby we need time to discuss it and thanked her for time. When they reached me, I was staring at the elevator doors with my arms folded.

"You'd think for millions of dollars this place would come equipped with a decent elevator." I pushed the button again.

"Assaulting that button the way you are won't make it get here any faster." Nathan held back a laugh as he took my hand. Gabby let a snort out and I shot her a look.

"Oh no." Gabby searched her pockets. "I forgot my phone inside. I need to get it and make sure everything is locked up, anyhow. It was a pleasure seeing you both again." She gave me a small smile and an almost nonexistent head nod before she turned to Nathan.

"If you have any questions or come to any decisions please don't hesitate to call me." She gave a flirty grin and hurried on back into the apartment.

The elevator ride was silent. The car ride home was awkward. The two flights of steps to the door of our place finally broke the silence.

"You know, that slow elevator was way quicker than this." Nathan grinned as he held the door open for me.

I smirked back at him, dropped my bag on the table, and plopped on the couch.

Nathan walked past me and into the kitchen.

I let out a huge sigh as a stress reliever, sprawled out on the couch, and propped myself up on my elbows.

"What are we going to do? I mean, I see nothing wrong with the brownstone on East 26th street. You didn't like that?" I sort of whined and begged at the same time.

"Jordan, it's the same size as this, twice the price, and our front door would still be on the street. Again. C'mon, you know why we're moving. I can't understand for the life of me why you're being so difficult." Nathan came out of the kitchen holding a bottle of water and sat down next to me.

I sat up all the way and leaned my head on his shoulder.

"You're right, I'm wrong. I'm sorry. I like the penthouse on Park Ave." I plucked a piece of lint off my shirt and looked at him. He had a shit-eating grin on his face.

"Say it again…" He chuckled.

"I like the penthouse on Park Avenue," I repeated.

"No, the part where you said I was right and you were…wait, what was that again? *Wrong?* Oh shit, someone please send the devil a parka because Hell just froze over" he teased.

"Oh, shut up."

I playfully shoved his shoulder and the next thing I knew he was on top of me, trying to grab my wrists. I tried to wriggle out and hold them above my head but I felt my back slide against the couch, and then we were on the floor. With his face buried in between my shoulder and neck, he began to kiss me.

He stopped suddenly and took my wrists in one hand while he propped himself up with the other. "What time will everyone be back?"

"Does it really matter at this point?"

I nudged my hips up with a small laugh. I could feel him against me.

"It just depends if I take you right here or if we're stripping on the way upstairs."

He sat up, pulled his shirt over his head, and tossed it over his shoulder. He hovered over me with the grin that made my heart pound and girl parts tingle. Yes, I said girl parts. Since having Nate, 'Mommy mode' was in full effect, so I wasn't only watching Disney Jr. but my language as well.

"I don't need my mom walking in on us. Especially with my kids in tow." He pulled the hem of my shirt up and ran his hands down over my breasts.

My hands immediately went in his hair, as he took full on advantage of my position. Finally, I found the air to ask what time it was.

"Unless you have a clock down here I have no idea and I don't care," he said while he kissed me and worked the button and zipper of my jeans.

"No, but I can see you do. What is that Big Ben you got in there?" I snickered playfully as I slid my hand down the front of him.

"My wifey is witty, gorgeous, and willing? Shit, I

hit the trifecta with you, baby," he teased me as he got on his knees and tugged off my boots and jeans.

I had no idea of the time, and to be honest I was beyond caring. I grabbed his belt and fumbled around with it until it was undone. The same went for his jeans. These days, everything was so rushed and chaotic that we never really had the time to do the spontaneous `hop on the counter and do me right now` thing anymore. It was nice to have a shot at getting rug burned again or breaking something and not worrying about it until later. I was just happy it was actually daylight and not in the bed. We had our showers though, so I shouldn't complain too much.

He still made my body tingle and I got lost whenever he touched me like that. Something about that carefree moment changed me. I think that's the moment I snapped out of my perpetual state of Grumparella, because I had it all, and if I were anyone else on the outside looking in I'd be calling myself a whiney selfish twat who had no idea how great her life was. The clothes came off quicker and the breathing got heavier. By the third growl, he had me bent over the side of the couch yanking on a fist full of my hair. *Jesus Christ I missed this.* I pushed back against him and turned around to face him. Somehow, we went from standing to me on top of him. Looks like I was getting that rug burn after all. Just as I was about to explode we heard the downstairs door slam shut. Emma and Fiona were talking as they walked up the steps. I heard Rachel laugh.

"Holy shit!"

Nathan busted out laughing as he reached for his jeans with me, still on top of him, trying to process what was happening because I was in a completely different zone just two seconds ago.

"Oh my god!" I jumped up as Nathan winced,

yanking his jeans over his dick that was still rock hard, with no boxers to protect him.

"Here." He tossed me his shirt since I couldn't find mine.

We were both laughing as we tried to make it around all the shit in the hallway to the upstairs.

"I've made it my entire life so far without my mother ever walking in on me and here I am at twenty-eight chafing my dick on jeans and yanking my wife up the steps behind me like a teenager," he muttered.

I laughed.

As we made it to the top of the steps, I heard the door open and Emma's backpack hit the floor with a thud, and then Rachel huffed about something. Fiona asked Emma to close the door in a hushed voice, plus Emma didn't call out for me, so I knew Nate must have been falling asleep or already asleep. Thank God because Nathan and I needed a quick shower, and not a cold one either. I heard my text message alert go off in our bedroom so I went in to get it. It was a text from Rachel.

> *Hey twat-muffin...you should pick up yours and your famous husband's skibbies off the floor before you scurry upstairs half neked. Or else next time I'll sell his on eBay. That's rent for like a year, ya know.*

I busted out laughing and texted her back.

> *Thanks hooch. We'll be down in a few...lol*

> *Yeah. OK. Ha Ha Ha. Make sure you ice that rug burn if I'm not here to remind you when you two get done. <3*

I grinned. Rachel knew me all too well.

Nathan pulled me into him from behind and began

kissing the exposed skin on my shoulder while he slid his hands up, taking my shirt along with them. I tossed my phone on the bed.

"Arms up." He nudged into me.

I lifted my arms above my head and he pulled my top off me. I turned around to face him. His pants were already undone and sliding down his legs.

"Woman, I will never get enough of you," he said as his mouth found my breasts.

He inched me back towards the bathroom as I kept my arms out behind me to feel for the walls and get a sense of direction.

Once we made it through the bathroom doors, I knew exactly where things were heading next. I hit play on the iPod player and then opened the shower door while he gripped my behind with one of his hands, as the other felt like it was everywhere at once. I reached in, turned the water on full blast, and waited for the steam. I loved the feel of him against me. I was thankful that this never got old. We were comfortable enough with one another to have no insecurities or care about anything else but the moment. He backed me into the shower and pulled the door shut. His lips never left mine.

The water poured over us, into our eyes and our mouths, while we devoured each other and his hand made his way down between my legs. Immediately, my head went back and I hiked my leg up where he held it up from behind my knee. I couldn't take much more. It had been a few weeks since we had this much alone time. I didn't want to rush but I knew we wouldn't last long.

I pushed off the wall with my free hand, moved it down, and wrapped it around him. That feeling alone could make me come, knowing I did that to him, that *we* together, turned him on that much. That was literally power in the palm of my hand. He buried his face between my neck and shoulder and alternated light bites and kisses while I worked him. He took in a sharp breath and I knew he was ready. He grabbed me by the back of my hair and commanded my body against the tile.

There he is, my take charge, I'm–going-to-fuck-you–seven-ways-to-Sunday Nathan and I couldn't be happier.

He palmed my breast and squeezed hard, then gave my nipple a teasing, long tug, and bending down for one last bite before he took me. And by the look in his eyes, I knew it was going to be a rough ride. The thought sent goose bumps all over, making every important part ready and willing as he jerked my right leg up under my knee, held up by the inside of his elbow and showed himself inside. He made a grand entrance, and he gave a whole new meaning to 'nailed my ass to the wall that's for sure' By that point, even the music playing couldn't drown out my screams of absolute pleasure, and neither of us could give two fucks who heard us.

He stopped and sat down on the built-in tiled ledge, or fuck seat as I called it, pulled me down to him by my hair and kissed me hard. *Fuck. Yes.*

He gripped my hips on both sides and I could feel where the blood was leaving from his fingerprints. I knew just what he wanted but I was going to make him wait for it. I grabbed the soap, and began to lather my hands. I turned, and bent over just enough to where I was exposed but he could see my face to the side, hair swaying back and forth upside down, as I slid my own hand between my legs. Nathan stiffened up even more and gripped me even tighter as I began to move. He kissed my behind as he slid two fingers into me and that was my undoing.

I crumbled around him for a moment, and when I finished he pulled me on top of him and let it all go. I rode him as he pounded into me, his face mashed into my back, right hand holding onto my hip for dear life with his other arm wrapped around touching me again. When he came, I could feel his body go limp and he pulled my head back to give me a long, passionate kiss.

"Mrs. Harper, do you have any idea how much I love you?"

He panted and dropped his hand down as I stood up.

"Well, I do know how much and I bet you anything the people across the street know it now, too." I laughed as I began to wash my hair.

He sat while I washed up and gave a hand with those hard to reach spots.

"I love you, Jordan." He kissed my forehead before I stepped out.

"I love you, too, Nathan." I smiled and let him clean up before there was no hot water left.

CHAPTER 4

Once we decided on where we were moving to, everything seemed to go a lot smoother and a lot less stressful. I *finally* hired a full staff at the bar so Rachel only had to go in at night to close and pay the bills. I'd to come to terms with the fact that I couldn't do it all. I had to let go of some things. While the bar was a huge part of me it was a part of me I could live without, but I couldn't live without Emma, Nathan, Nate, or Rachel, so I had to pick my battles. The bar it was. I mean, I still owned it; Rachel was just head honcho now. Amber was still there; in fact, she'd beefed up those titties of hers with a boob job. They looked nice and felt surprisingly real.

Don't ask.

Rachel and I grilled about fifty applicants until we came up with the lucky number seven to hire. The post now had ten employees, and one owner. I was impressed. It was like a real grown up place to work now. Complete with schedules and all. *Ugh. Now I have to make schedules?* So with the bar covered, I had plenty of time to focus on the move and my family.

Nathan was going to have to go to LA for a few weeks the next month so two big things needed to happen before then. The first, Nathan needed a new assistant. Lila didn't want to leave Los Angeles. Nathan couldn't blame her. That's where her family lived. He understood. The second was trying desperately to get the closing on the penthouse ASAP so he'd be here for the move. There were people that were coming to pack up the entire apartment, but I just didn't feel right about having some stranger pack up our personal crap. So I did the personal stuff like clothing, pictures, and our laptops, not to mention some sensitive security footage. Okay, well it wasn't exactly 'security footage'. It was more like good cop dirty cop in the bedroom type of footage.

What?

Don't judge me. My husband always looked like the sexy man beast he is on the screen. No matter what role he was playing. I didn't look too bad myself.

Anyhow, it wasn't like I didn't have the free time to do that stuff, so I took on the tasks. Nathan's parents would come and take Nate every morning for a walk, get themselves some coffee and a stroll through a park. They alternated their spots. In the few hours they had him, I worked my ass off. Usually the first hour Nathan was working *my* ass off...off the counter...off the couch...off the rooftop. You get the point. I was so happy things were getting back to normal. I knew once we got moved and settled in it would be back to a hundred percent. No chaos, no tripping over stuff in the halls, and no more paps camped out on my stoop. We were in the home stretch on the road to drama-free land.

Close to a week later, we closed and started the

move.

"I'm going to miss this place," Emma said, hugging me around my waist.

"Are you now? I thought you hated the steps, and all the noise at night? You going to miss that too?" I laughed as I kissed the top of her head.

She looked up at me with the most serious face I'd ever seen and she said to me, "This has been the only place I've known my entire life, Mom, I don't even know if I'll be able to sleep at night without those noises. They've become a part of me, and I'm scared this new place will never compare to this one."

She meant it. Whatever anxiety Emma was having about moving, it was real, and I had to help her move past it quickly.

"Em, we're not selling this place. I promise you, I'll keep this building until the day I die and then you'll get it. Shit, when you're ready to go out on your own, this will be here for you, baby." I tried to reassure her.

"Really? You'd let me live here when I turn eighteen?" Her eyes lit up and excitement rang through her voice.

"Well, I said when you're ready, not when you turn eighteen, and I promise to charge you half of the going rental prices." I nudged her.

"Ha ha ha, rent, yeah right. You wouldn't do that to me. Would you?" She looked up at me with uncertainty in her eyes.

"Yup, unless you're in college full-time. Then you can live here rent-free. Deal?" I stuck out my pinky.

"Deal," she said, latching her pinky with mine.

Emma and Nathan took some personal stuff over to the new place, and I stayed behind while the last of our stuff was loaded on the truck. Plus, I needed to do a quick run through to make sure everything was out, and shut off the main breaker either until I got it rented out or winter came.

I stood in the middle of the empty room and spun around slowly, checking out every corner, every mark on the wall, and every scuff on the floor. Each of them had a memory. I couldn't believe this was it. I never thought I'd ever see the day, yet here it was. There was one last stop on memory lane before I locked up and headed out. I ran upstairs, flung open the bedroom window, and headed to the rooftop. I stood against the wall and took in one last look at the gorgeous view. I realized I was standing in the exact spot where Nathan and I first kissed. Suddenly the thought entered my mind that maybe I wouldn't miss this place as much as I thought I would because truth be told as long as I had my family, I could live anywhere.

Speaking of family, my sister Kelly was so excited we were moving to Park Avenue. She insisted they had the cutest doormen. Cuter than on any other block. She was such a loon. When I walked over to the rooftop entrance door to make sure it was secured, and locked, I noticed a pack of cigarettes sitting there. Nathan must have left them up here before he quit. Which was only recently, so I picked up the pack of smokes and took them downstairs with me. I locked up the rest of the place and headed outside.

I sat on the front stoop and pulled out the cigarettes. It had a pack of matches inside the cellophane, so I figured, ah what the hell. What's one for old time sake? I took out a smoke and struck the match to light it. I expected that first inhale to be heavenly. Holy shit, was I wrong. I coughed and completely ruined my obligatory, sentimental goodbye moment.

I stared at the lit stink stick and let out a small laugh as I butted it out just as Frank pulled up to the curb.

"Tsk tsk, young lady." He laughed.

"Well shit, you caught me. I was trying to have a

Sex in the City kind of moment. You know, saying goodbye all cool and calm with a smoke. A 'thanks for the memories, kid' type of deal." I laughed at Frank's expression. It was a cross between a `what the fuck' and `have you lost your shit?' face.

"Aw, c'mon. Cut me some slack. I'm really going to miss this place." I stood up and brushed off my butt.

"Really, Jordie? What will you miss most about it? The place where your `look, honey, I'm not really dead' psycho ex-husband nearly killed Nathan, or the rooftop?" He snickered as he put my bag over his shoulder, handed me my purse and then picked up the last box to put it in the car.

"Well, when you put it like that, I sound like a selfish asshole." I yanked the car door open and sat down in a huff.

"Thanks," I mumbled and closed the door.

When we pulled away, I watched in the side view mirror until I couldn't see the bar sign or apartment any longer. I really didn't live there anymore.

We drove in silence for a few minutes. The clouds in the sky moved in the opposite direction we did and when we ended up stuck in traffic, I squirmed uncomfortably. What Frank had said bothered the shit out of me.

"Why would you say that to me?" I blurted out.

Dammit. I shouldn't have said that out loud.

"Why did I say what, Jordan?" Frank looked over his shoulder before pulling into the next lane. Horns were blaring all around us and suddenly, it was like a scene from a movie. Gridlock had me trapped in an uncomfortable situation.

Yay, me.

"Why would you bring up what happened to Nathan in the apartment?"

"Why wouldn't I?" He laid on the horn and called

the cabbie trying to inch in front of us a piece of shit.

"Jesus, Frank, I'm not in the mood for a mind fuck today. Why did you mention it? We don't talk about it. You know that." I shifted in my seat so my back was against the door and I could face him.

"Just because *you* don't talk about it doesn't mean it didn't' happen," he spit out and then immediately began cursing and honking the horn again like a lunatic.

"FRANK!" I yelled, "What the hell is wrong with you?"

"Jordie, sometimes I wonder how someone so intelligent and street smart can also put on the blinders to the shit you don't want to see." He stared at me as if he was waiting for a response and when I closed my mouth, he shook his head and gave a short sarcastic laugh. "Figured as much."

He looked straight ahead out into the traffic, and I turned and went back to facing forward in my seat. We sat silent again for a few minutes and it was hard as a mofo to hold back the tears, but I did. They were angry tears, and he wasn't going to get to see a single one of them.

"What's your deal, Frank?"

"My deal, Jordan? Well, *my deal* is that as of late, it's been a lot about you and what you need and what's wrong with you, and a lot less of you caring what Nathan needs." He wasn't talking to me; he was talking *down* to me.

"Excuse me?" I went back at him immediately on the defense, and then took in a deep breath to try to think about what was about to fly out of my mouth because after I said it there was no taking it back. "Look, I get it. You're protective of him–"

"Of *all* of you, Jordie," he interrupted.

"Okay, fine, of *all* of us. But whatever you're

thinking isn't fair or true. We've been to hell and back, mister, and if you think..."

"You know what I think? I think you need to take a good look at what's been happening. You give that boy a hard time about everything. You can't just let go...you can never just say all right, let's do that, or yes, thank you for letting me sleep. He goes to change the baby's diaper and you swoop in like he isn't capable—"

"Not true! I do those things because I don't want him to have to work all day or night and come home to do *my job*. It's my job to keep him happy. What kind of wife would I be if I allowed my husband to work all the goddamned time and have to come home and take care of kids, too? I'd be a shitty one."

"No, you'd be a *human*. You can't do it all, all the time, Jordie. He *wants* to help, and you make him feel like shit half the time barging in and taking over. And let's be honest, it's not like he's out there doing manual labor eighteen hours a day, Jordan. So I think he'd be okay with feeding his son dinner, or changing a few shitty diapers. Hell, you fought with him about moving out of your place. Think about that for a second. The most traumatic place in the world for him, and yet he stayed, didn't he? Why? Because you, Nate, and Emma are *everything* to him. He would rather relive the pain of what he went through and lost that day Jason nearly killed him than leave your side." He slammed his fist on the dashboard and I flinched.

"And that, Jordan, *is my deal*."

Holy shitbricks, that son of a bitch was right. I effed up royally and I didn't know how to even begin to try to fix it.

CHAPTER 5

When we pulled up to the building—ugh, when we pulled up to 'our new home,'—a young man opened the door for me and Frank immediately jumped out like a mad man and ran around the front of the car to my side.

"I don't know if you didn't get the memo kid, but me or one of my men are the only people allowed to open these doors," Frank yelled at the poor guy as an older man approached them and began to apologize. He looked to be in his sixties and had a heavy Italian accent.

"I'm so sorry, Frank, forgive me, I had to use the restroom. The kid is new. He didn't know who was in the car." He took his doorman hat off and held it across his chest nodding his head like he was bowing or some shit to Frank. The new guy looked like he might need a fresh pair of boxers after the way Frank went after him.

"It won't happen again. I promise, Frank." The older gentleman held out his hand to help me out of the car.

"Thank you. And please, excuse Frank. He's a bit on the cranky side today." I gave the old man a grin.

When we walked into the new place, it was exciting, refreshing, and overwhelming all at once. I busted out in tears.

"Holy shit, she hasn't even made it through the door and she's a nightmare." I heard Rachel's voice come from somewhere behind the wall of boxes in the living area.

"Be nice, Rachel. She's under a lot of stress." I heard Nathan say as he walked down the hallway towards me, wearing my smile.

When he reached me, he took my purse and set it down on the floor, wrapped his arms around me, and kissed the top of my head while I sobbed.

"What's going on? You okay?"

I could tell he was humoring me, not asking me. Which made me feel ridiculous, so I laughed and looked up at him.

"I'm fine. Frank yelled at me though. I think we should talk later." I sniffled and wiped my face on his shirt.

Nathan gave a laugh while he thanked me for using his shirt as a towel then bent down and kissed me. He pushed all his weight against me until I was against the doorjamb.

"Oh Christ, I didn't yell at you, Jordie. I was talking loud that's all," Frank said as he tried to squeeze past us through the doorway.

"Holy hell, you two. Seriously?" Rachel scoffed as she attempted to get the tape off a box marked 'miscellaneous.'

"I'm bound and determined to find my Michael Kors bag, you sticky fingered bitch," she mumbled playfully.

"Nuh-uh! You did so yell at me and then you went

postal on the poor door guy for doing his job." I sniffled again.

"Joseph? Frank, you got into it with a grandpa. Did you steal his lunch money, too, you big bully?" Nathan laughed as he let go of me and slapped Frank on the shoulder. "I don't know, old man, you're getting kind of crotchety in your years, eh?"

Frank shook his head and gave me the 'get your shit together' look. Ugh, he wasn't going to let this go.

"Come on, I'll show you what we got set up so far."

Nathan took my hand and led me down the hallway where just before I turned the corner I stuck my tongue out at Frank and smirked. I didn't wait for his reaction. I didn't really care about it anyhow. I knew he was right.

"Hey, if something was bothering you, you'd tell me, right?" I asked Nathan just before we got to Emma's room.

"What? Oh yeah, sure I would. Okay, here's Emma's room." He pulled me through the doorway.

"I need to talk to you." I tugged on his hand to stop him from dragging me in any further.

"What's up?" He looked around the room wide-eyed and smiling, then down at me.

I realized that his eyes hadn't been that bright blue in a few weeks. Not just bright blue color-wise, the excitement was back in them.

"Thank you. Thank you for everything. Thank you for our son, and accepting Emma as your own. Thank you for putting up with me when I turn into an emotional fruitcake. Thank you for coming home every night to my shitty apartment, even though what happened to you there was god-awful. I'm so sorry I've been a selfish, emotional, borderline tyrant. Just, thank you for everything. I love you *so very much,* Nathan, and I've been the stupidest bitch on the planet. I was trying so hard to make sure I didn't lose you by being a slacker or asking you to help with the baby or with dinner. I took over...everything. I'm sorry. Please forgive me?" I looked up at him all bleary-eyed and gave a big sniffle.

"Woman, stop with the tears. I love you. Nothing needs to be forgiven. Look where we're standing. This is a second chance for both of us to be a part of something amazing. Us, our kids, my mom and dad, Tyler, and I guess even Rachel..." He nodded his head back and smiled.

"I heard that, asshole, Rachel yelled from the front room."

"Ah damn, the baby monitor is on in Nate's room." He remembered.

We both laughed and I stood up on my tippy toes to give him a kiss. "I don't know what I did to deserve you."

"If I had to guess, I'd say probably because you endured life with that criminally insane ex-husband of yours."

He opened Emma's closet. All her clothes were already unpacked and hung up or placed in her dresser drawers. Her room was pretty much done except the two boxes of personal stuff in the corner. Nathan figured it'd be best for her to do that herself.

"It looks amazing, Nathan. She is going to *love* it."

"Come on. Nate's room is finished, and ours is just about done. Let me show you." He took my hand.

Just as we made it into the hallway, we heard Rachel's voice, very loud and very slowly.

"What. The. *Fuck*? Jordan, seriously bitch, you gone and lost your damn mind. What is all this?"

She was still shouting when we walked into the front room.

"What are you yelling about?" Frank asked as all

three of us came to stand by her.

There it was, in all its glory—the box marked 'Personal Do Not Touch. Especially YOU, Rachel!'

The box just sat there, wide open, along with Rachel's mouth. She slowly raised her arms and turned to face us holding a pair of white panties with 'Mrs. Harper' slapped across the ass in bright red letters.

Nathan shrugged his shoulders.

"What's the big deal? She *is* Mrs. Harper. She just labeled her undies on the outside instead of on the tag?" He paused. "Okay, yeah, what gives?"

Rachel stood frozen staring at me in mock horror and confusion because she knew what Nathan didn't.

"Oh, it's a big deal all right." She snickered when she threw the panties at me and I busted out laughing again.

"This! It's literally 'a big deal,'" Rachel confirmed, reading the packing slip aloud.

"What? Is it a crime for me to *really* like something?" I tried to get the paper from her.

"Oh Jesus, I can't stand when you two doubletalk all cryptic and shit. It's like a different frequency that only you two can hear." Nathan got to the paper first and scanned the invoice.

"Wow, I'd say at a dollar each you got the best deal ever, considering these things retail for about fifteen bucks a pop." He shook his head and smiled as he wrapped his arms around me and kissed my forehead.

I squinted at him. "I may or may not be disturbed that you know that."

"Like you're one to judge right now?" Frank scoffed.

"Cool it, big guy. We had a chat, didn't we? No need to be nasty anyhow. I know you mean well…" Nathan patted Frank on the back.

"It's more like he *does* mean well, because he really does. He's one mean mother effer when he wants to be. That's for sure."

"All right, enough, both of you, please. Not in front of the kids," Nathan's mom said as she walked through the still open front door. "I could hear all your shenanigans from the elevator hall. You have neighbors now. Not many but you do, so zip it." She handed me Nate.

"Hi Em." I bent down to give Emma a kiss.

"Hi." She gave me a quick peck and took off for her room yelling, "Bye."

"Honey, he may need a diaper change," Fiona said to me as she handed me the diaper bag.

"Yeah, that kid was fartin' up a storm on the cab ride over," Nathan's dad chuckled.

"I'll get it, Jordie." Nathan reached for the bag and instinctively pulled back.

"No, I can…" I began.

Nathan's expression changed for a split second, and suddenly it was so obvious that I hurt him every time I denied him. I mean yeah, it may have been denying him a shitty diaper but I still was denying him.

"I can't hand you the bag and him at the same time. Here take him first." I handed him Nate and then the bag. "Have fun with that. In the meantime I've got a thousand panties with my name on them to remove from the living room before anyone else sees them," I whispered in his ear and smacked his ass playfully.

"Frank, a hand please?" I asked the big bad security specialist with an attitude problem, as I stood over the box.

"Yeah, close it up first though." He nearly cracked a smile. That was a good sign.

"Alright party people, I'm outta' here. Tyler will be home soon and I wanna be there when he gets back."

Rachel said before hugging me. She then made her way to Nathan's parents for a farewell before she took off.

"Bye, biiiiitt…uh bye, Jords." She waved and closed the door behind her.

No more calling each other 'bitches and hoes'…and the one I miss the most, no more 'hollers'.' It was like salt in the wound. It had saved our lives, when my assumed dead turned terrorist ex-husband Jason was about to kidnap Emma and kill me off, but it burned like a mofo. So, we just phased it out of our vocabulary. My guess would be that at this point, the fairy tale was over and reality was setting in. The first order of business on the agenda of reality was dealing with Frank.

"Thanks," I said to Frank after he put the box up on the top shelf of my ridiculously huge closet.

"No problem." He was curt.

"Really, Frank, I don't know what more I can do for you at this moment. I had a talk with Nathan. I apologized, and I let him change a diaper full of shit," I whined.

"That's a good start, Jordan." He turned to walk out.

"Hey, what is really bothering you, Frank?" I tugged on the arm of his shirt lightly.

"What isn't bothering me, Jordie? Look at everything changing, overnight. Now that you kids live up here you won't be needing me around as much. My daughter starts college in three months and will be living in the city. She won't want me around nor will she need me around."

"First of all, of course we'll still need you. Secondly, of course, your daughter will still need you. And third, would it be *so* bad to go back to LA and retire? Travel with Annie. I mean she's been one hell of a patient wife for all of these years." I nudged his arm. "You know, get in some 'Frankie loves Annie' alone time. And who knows, maybe when you guys are done traveling the world you can come try out a residency on the east coast. We aren't *all* that bad over here after all."

"You're a good kid, Jordan. I'm sorry about earlier. It wasn't my place…"

"Fuhgettabout it." I winked. "It's your place to say whatever you want. You've kept him safe all those years before I came into the picture and then some afterwards."

I linked my arm with his and led him towards the hallway.

"Not safe enough…I…" He stopped talking.

I patted his hand and left my hand over his as we walked down the hallway.

"If I don't get to blame myself, you sure as hell can't blame yourself. Nobody was prepared for what happened to him. *Nobody*." I knew exactly what he was thinking.

He stopped and put his other hand on top of mine and made a Frank hand sandwich.

"Are we okay now?" His eyes crinkled a bit and the stress lines on his forehead were predominant.

"We are as long as nobody finds out about that box of panties up there." I tossed my head back in the direction of the closet.

"I know a guy who can sell them on the street if you're that hard up for cash, lady." He nudged me as we walked into the hallway.

We stopped at the baby's room and saw Nathan had just finished changing Nate's diaper. He picked his son up off the changing table with his back to us. He began moving him up and down in front of him, making a swoosh sound with each movement. I got nervous and right away went towards him in a panic, but I stopped myself when I saw Nate's smile at his daddy as he flew through the air.

Everything is going to be all right.

CHAPTER 6

We finally got settled in over the last few weeks, things were getting back to normal. Whatever our normal was. It was hard with Nathan gone for thirteen days, but I managed. Rachel and Tyler came and stayed a night or two while he was away. Fiona took Nate on both the weekends that Nathan wasn't home, and Emma went to Kelly's so I decided to work at the bar. I'd missed it and Rachel deserved a break. She only bartended Friday and Saturday nights mostly, but still went in nightly to close up, and did payroll once a week. Besides, everyone loved a surprise visit from the boss every now and again. Right?

When I got there, the line was a typical Friday night line—halfway down the block. I had to squeeze between the railing and people to get to Mike, but I could finally see his bald head above the crowd. A group of women inched over towards the railing, and one of them made a snide remark about me cutting. I threw her a dirty look and she handed me one right back.

Oh shit, am I out of bitch practice or what?

"Excuse me," I said to the one who jabbed me with the not so subtle elbow to my rib cage.

"Right, bitch. Whateva'. You ain't getting in before me. Do you even know who I am?" She had a thick Spanish accent, and she was absolutely beautiful but her attitude sucked.

"Apparently you don't know who I am and you aren't getting in here at all. Hey, Mike! Over here!" I jumped up and down to get his attention because they weren't letting me over that railing.

"I'm Bristol Santana's personal assistant. She is personal friends with the owner and his baby mamma." She tossed her hair.

"Uh, what?" I'd heard what she said but I needed to hear it again to believe it.

"Yeah the owner, Nate Harper, and his kid's motha'. Why am I even explaining this to you?" She snapped her fingers in the air to Mike and I could see him roll his eyes and ignore her.

I stood on the bottom of the railing and waved frantically again. "Miiiike!" I flailed, this time getting his attention and a smile.

"Excuse me…" Ms. Assistant began to say but Mike moved past her to grab me by under my arms. He lifted me over the rail, keeping me in a bear hug.

"Jords! I haven't seen you in forever, Jesus Christ," he yelled over the noise coming from inside when someone came through the door.

"Hold that thought." I put my finger up to him as he put me down. I turned to Ms. Assistant and introduced myself.

"I'm Jordan Harper, *owner* of this establishment and the *wife* of Nathan Harper. I'm not quite sure where you get your info from but tell your source they'd better watch their mouth. Now you can turn your pretty, little ass around and leave. Please, don't ever come back. Tell Ms. Santana that if she wishes to come speak with me or make prior arrangements to come hang out here, please do so with one of my staff members so we can make sure she gets everything she needs. We don't have a VIP room here. It's pretty basic, so we couldn't offer her privacy. FYI. Now go. Buh-bye."

I waved her off as Mike began to herd them out of the line.

"You wait til Bristol finds out, she's gonna' be pissed off. Stupid bitch, don't know what you're getting yourself caught up in." She was still shouting as Mike escorted her away. I laughed and waited for him to get them to the street.

When he got back, Mike gave me another hug with a huge smile. "What are you doing here?"

"I had a night to myself, so I decided to come check it out. See how things are going, you know." I shrugged.

"Yeah, okay, Ms. Innocent 'ya know' shoulder shrug. You miss being behind the bar and you miss us." He gave my shoulder a light 'aw shucks' type of punch.

"Yeah yeah, whatever." I rolled my eyes and smirked. "You need to come by the new place to have dinner and see the baby. He's getting big," I shouted as I counted five people that walked out. Mike counted the next four people in line and let them in.

"I'm going to get inside. I'll see you later." I nudged him with my shoulder as I walked past him. He just laughed and I could feel his eyes on me as I went inside. Jesus Christ, what a zoo. It had been over a year since I was behind the bar on a night like this, and for whatever reason it scared the shit out of me. I suddenly felt like I couldn't breathe and I was trapped.

What the fuck, is this a panic attack? Just as I turned, I bumped chest to chest with Carlos who was another man in my life that could pick me up like a rag doll, swing me around and squeeze me to death.

"Jordie!" He seemed genuinely excited to see me. That eased up my nerves a bit.

"Hey buddy, long time." I smiled and hugged him back after my feet hit the floor.

"Listen, think you can get me up to the bar in one piece? I'm a bit rusty," I admitted sheepishly.

"Oh hell yeah, I can. Hop on!" He turned around and patted his back.

"What? No, you aren't giving me a piggy back ride." I laughed.

"Suit yourself, I gave you an option. Now it's my way." He grinned.

Before I could even respond, he bent and slung me over his shoulder, ass in the air, and made his way to the bar. Once we reached it, he sat me down on it. I turned but when I saw the hustling behind the bar, it hit me like a goddamn ton of bricks. I wasn't missed one bit back there. They were getting along just fine. In fact, those two looked like Rachel and I did not too long ago. I would just be in the way if I went back there. They seemed to have everything running smoothly, people were happy, and drinks were getting poured one after another. Just as I went to hop down, Amber caught the back of my shirt and pulled me back.

"Oh my god! How are you?" She yelled over the music and hugged me from behind. "You want some of this?" She jacked her thumb over her shoulder and smiled. "I could use an expert's hand tonight. Some of these guys are pretty ornery."

She adjusted her boobs, looked up at me, and smiled. "They look good right? They finally dropped and settled. Feel them." She stuck her chest out.

I busted out laughing and respectfully declined.

"I'll definitely feel you up when the place isn't jam packed." I swung my legs over the bar. Chelsey, who was one of the newer employees, smiled and reached past me.

We never did get to talk much, which felt odd because this place was my life for so long. I'd had my hands in everything when it came to this bar, and now, not only were the faces unfamiliar but so was the whole damn place. I realized at that moment, I had moved on from this part of my life and nothing would ever be the same as it was pre-Nathan. Everything had changed fundamentally and permanently…but I couldn't have been happier.

I saw Rachel round the side of the bar with some ice. She dropped it as soon as she caught a glimpse of me.

"Biiiiotch!" She slapped my leg then pulled me off and behind the bar. "What are you doing here, fucker? I thought you'd be watching *The Real Housewives of New Jersey* or some shit from the deluxe apartment in the sky-y-y-y," she teased.

"What the fuck ever." I rolled my eyes, and laughed, as I grabbed the bucket of ice and filled the bay up.

"It's nice to have you here. I've missed you…whore." She winked at me and teetered across the floor to some guy who looked as if he was about to spontaneously combust from yelling so much to get any one of our attentions for a drink.

I got back into the rhythm of things quicker than I thought I would, and well, pretty soon it became the Jordie and Rachel show all over again. Regulars were coming up and chit-chatting, asking how I'd been, how were the baby and Emma. I found it so funny that not one of the male customers asked about Nathan.

Men. About an hour later, I noticed Amber on the floor with a tray taking orders and Chelsea cleaning tables up.

"I feel bad I showed up now," I shouted to Rachel and nodded in their direction.

"Why? If anything, you're making it easier on them. They're getting more shit done being on the floor than back here. Everything they're cleaning up now, they don't have to clean up later. Plus, look at Amber—taking orders, coming back here making them herself. Pretty fucking efficient if you ask me. I'm happy you're here." She uncapped three beers and poured seven shots.

When she turned her attention back to the customer, I handed one of the regulars his beer.

"It's on me Ben, good to see you again." I smiled at him and got a wink in return before he walked off. I grabbed the rag to wipe up the mess Rachel had left from the obnoxious amount of shots she just poured. Someone started shouting something at me.

"Oh girrrrlllll, if drinks are on you then pour me two more," she said in a southern twang I would recognize anywhere.

Naomi? What the...? She should be with Nathan in LA.

I looked up and smiled at her, because no matter how much she thought she blended in, the woman just stuck out like a gorgeous sore thumb. Naomi owned a room when she walked in. I couldn't pinpoint one thing about her that turned *everybody's* attention to her. She just had it all.

"What are you doing here? I thought you were in LA with Nathan? Is everything okay?" My voice got higher and higher as I rattled off the questions, and she laughed at me.

"Everything is perfectly fine, gorgeous. Just got

done a few days early is all. Now can a girl get a drink at this rodeo or what?" She smacked her hand on the bar with a smile.

"What can I get ya?" I had to practically scream back to ask her even though she was in my face. The crowd had jacked up about three decibels in just a few moments time.

"How about a shot of Southern Comfort and a Manhattan to chase it down with. A little bit of then and now. And pour yourself one while you're at it. Let's celebrate being two bitches out on the town." She grinned.

"Sure thing." I laughed and grabbed some shot glasses and the bottle of Southern Comfort. When I turned back around I caught a glimpse of a group of people obviously checking something out so I asked Naomi to hang on a sec I wanted to find out what it was. If there was a fight brewing, I wasn't having that shit. When I hopped on the bar to get a look, I noticed people taking pics and then I saw him. He was home, my husband, my Nathan. I was so happy I screamed his name at the top of my lungs but he couldn't hear me.

"Why didn't you tell me he came back with you?" I said to Naomi, who by this time had poured her own shots.

"I think he wanted to surprise you. Although, he wasn't too happy when he got home and nobody was there, and then you didn't answer your cell. He knew where you'd be and he asked if I wanted to come with. So, here I am."

I chuckled at Naomi and looked back up to see if I could get Nathan's attention when I noticed he was standing taking pictures with the same chick. One after another, everyone was taking pics of them. Then I noticed something else. The bitch I threw out of line,

Bristol Santana's assistant, was standing next to them holding the other chick's purse.

W. T. F.

I hopped off the bar and pushed through the crowd. When I got behind them, I stuck my head between and pushed through with my back turned toward little miss-up-and-comer, Bristol Santana.

"Babe!" Nathan grabbed me around the waist and pulled me in tight.

"Jesus Christ, did I miss you," he said before he devoured my face in a jam-packed public place, and I loved every minute of it. When we finally came up for air, he introduced me to Bristol. I was very cordial but I felt the need to let her know I didn't want her assistant in my bar.

I leaned in and told her semi privately, "I'm sorry to have to bring this up but I told your assistant right there that she wasn't welcome in my bar. Not only did she throw an elbow in my ribs but she also dropped your name, called me a bitch, and Nathan's baby mamma. My bouncer out front knew that, so I'm not quite sure how she even got by him."

The entire bar didn't need to know that she had a rude ass assistant.

"She did? Seriously?" She asked, appalled.

"Yeah, but no big deal. It's over with now." I could see she was pissed so I tried to save face at that point, but I was too late.

"Evie, did you disrespect Nathan's wife?" She grabbed Evie by the arm and spun her around to face her. Evie looked over to me with that deer in the headlights glaze over and then back to Bristol.

"Yes, but I didn't—" she began, but was cut off.

"But nothing. You know my grandmother had an old saying. 'Anything after but is bullshit', and I know you aren't going to call my granny a liar now are you?

Get out of here. You're fired," Bristol said to her, stone faced.

Holy shit she just totally Donald Trumped her, like it was nothing. "Oh my god, no, Bristol you didn't have to do–" I started to say.

"I didn't have to do what? Fire her? Of course I did. There's only room for one bitch on this ride, and that's me." She flashed what could be mistaken for a grin of hostile sorts, but I chose to think it was a friendly reminder of who she was in the scheme of things. I was not as subtle on the other hand.

"All right then. It was nice to meet you. Take care now." I gave her a fake Miss Debutant smile while I pulled Nathan by his arm away from the crowd around us.

That's when it actually dawned on me who she was. She was the up and coming Bristol Santana. The young one from the red carpet that said she would love to work with Nathan. Ugh.

Nathan totally derailed my thoughts when he picked me up and sat me on the side of the bar. He pushed between my legs and pulled my head down to him by the back of my hair.

Bristol who? Tonight was going to be a good one.

CHAPTER 7

I went back to say bye to Rachel and everyone else before pulling Naomi off the stage to tell her we were leaving. When I saw Naomi was busy dancing with some guy I just signaled to the door and waved goodbye. She nodded and waved and motioned like she'd text me. I nodded back and Nathan led the way out. Carlos made a path for us to walk in front but when there was a sudden hand on my shoulder from behind, I jumped and let out a startled scream.

" It's just me kiddo." Frank gave a small smile.

"Jesus, Frank!" As I turned back, I saw Bristol watching us leave. She gave me a sly smirk and a four finger wave. I saw Nathan look over, she immediately perked up and gave a full wave goodbye accompanied by a million dollar smile.

"I don't like that bitch," I said to Nathan through the fake smile plastered on my face because she was still staring at us. He laughed as we got to the door and things started to quiet down. Carlos shook Nathan and Frank's hands, then gave me a hug.

"It's good to see ya, boss lady. I know it must be hard to make the trip from the Uppa' East Siiiide to us Village folk," he teased.

"Whatever." I smacked his arm.

"Nah, I'm just playin'. I hope you know that. I'm happy for you. We're all happy for you." He pointed his chin towards the bar.

Mike gave me a hug goodbye and shook Nathan's hand, which I know is hard for him because he isn't Nathan's biggest fan. I don't think he knew I was aware how he felt, but I did, and I admired him for always being so cordial. When we got to the sidewalk, I stopped and looked left. As I stared at our old place, I let out an involuntary sigh.

"Want to go check it out? Make sure everything is all right in there? No leaky pipes or anything?" Nathan asked.

"Nah, it's okay. I'm just so happy you're home early." I gave him a sheepish smile, locked my hand with his, and started towards the car waiting for us at the curb. He stood stationary and tugged me back to him. It tripped me up for a second but I caught my footing pretty quick.

"What are you doing?" I laughed when he pulled me to his chest and looked down at me.

"You know, not *all* bad happened there." He flashed me a 'nut-job' smile and I just about melted.

"I know."

"Hold on, I have an idea." He motioned to Frank that we'd be a minute and I saw Frank roll his eyes and get back in the car. "Okay, humor me. Stand here and count to twenty then walk to the stoop. When you get there you'll know what to do." He grinned.

"Nathan, no, really…" I began but he was already walking backwards smiling so hard it made *my* cheeks hurt.

"Count," he ordered me with a chuckle.

I must have looked pretty fucking stupid standing in the middle of the sidewalk smiling and counting out loud.

"Seventeen, eighteen, nineteen, twenty. Ready or not here I come," I said quietly as I began walking towards our old building.

Then I saw him. He was sitting on the steps just like that first night. He was right. I knew what to do.

"Fuck," I blurted out, as I got closer to him.

"Is that a statement or a request?" He grinned.

"Oh, that's a promise, Mr. Harper." I went straight to him and straddled him on the steps.

"Wow, I'm impressed. You brushed up on those flirting skills, didn't you?" he teased.

"I love you," I said and then mouthed the words 'nut-job'.

He busted out laughing and pulled me in closer.

"I love you, too, Mrs. Harper."

Just as he landed a quick kiss on my nose, the noise level began to rise. "Shit, and so it begins," I said and climbed off him. "To be continued..."

"Um, yeah, right there in that car." He nodded at the parked car.

"Yeah, right. Cranky Franky won't have any hanky panky happening on his shift. Besides, you know he gets all bent about how others have to sit on those seats." I laughed as I pulled his hand to help him up.

I realized then, the elevated crowd noise was still over by the bar and nobody was near us. We stopped at the edge of the sidewalk and could see Mike and Carlos trying to break the crowd up. I caught a glimpse of Bristol in the middle. When it started to look like it was getting out of hand, Frank hopped out to help. Once he made it through the crowd, he gave Mike enough room to pick Bristol up and literally throw her over his shoulder. He carried her through the crowd with Carlos in front of him, and Frank behind him until they reached her car.

By that time, Nathan and I were by our car watching the whole thing. I saw something in Bristol's body language when she reached up, kissed Mike on the cheek then touched his face and thanked him.

"Oh Jesus, she sure is one hell of an actress with that Gone with the Wind bullshit, heartfelt, dramatic, damsel-in-distress thank you." I snickered.

"Okay, first off, that was a mouthful." He laughed. "And second, I'm pretty sure that was sincere. She has horrible anxieties about being trampled, or trapped by a crowd. When she was like ten or something she was trapped in a moving crowd in Italy and separated from her parents for hours."

"Sucks for her," I mumbled and got into the car.

I didn't like her, and I certainly didn't like the way she looked at Mike.

When we pulled up to our building, the doorman didn't even look our way until I said hello to him. As we walked past him, I heard Frank say something about keeping his eyes forward.

"All right, you two, I'm headed out. If you need me, you know where I'll be."

"Wait, Frank, do you want to come up for coffee?" I asked and Nathan nudged me in the back.

I didn't look back at him. I just gave him a quick nonchalant nudge back with my foot.

Frank laughed and declined. Said he was tired and going to try to get some paper work finished. He was selling the Middletown office to one of his men who retired from the Navy.

"Thank you though Jordan. I won't intrude on anymore of your guys' time. I'm thankful you two waited until you were out of the car, at least." He chuckled and nodded his head goodbye.

"See you two Sunday."

I guess he knew since we had the place to ourselves the rest of the weekend we wouldn't be going anywhere. Frank scored an A+ in the intuitive department.

One of the bad things about living in a building like ours, especially at times like this, was the elevator ride. It was damned near unbearable because of the cameras. It seemed like the longest ride *ever* while you waited with anticipation to get fucked seven ways 'til Sunday. But then again, the cameras could only catch so much.

As soon as we got in, Nathan led me against the wall under the camera hole and pressed against me. Camera or not, in a minute it wouldn't have mattered because we would have fogged up the lens. Evidently, the ride up is much quicker when you're pre-occupied. We got out of the elevator and literally kissed our way to the apartment door. He slammed me up against it, still kissing me as he dug in his jeans pocket for his keys.

Once inside, we fumbled and stumbled our way around the apartment, leaving a piece of clothing at every bump. It was nothing like the choreographed love scenes you see in the movies. It was way better. It was the all-over-the-place, hanging-and-sliding-off-things, 'I'll be sore for the next five days,' 'is someone being bludgeoned to death in there?' kind of lovin'.

When we finished up round one an hour later with a quick shower, we headed up to give the new rooftop a try. I wasn't allowed up there until Nathan was finished whatever project he was working on, and lord knows it took him long enough but it was well worth the wait. Nothing could have prepared me for what I saw. Nothing. Aside from the wall and view being considerably higher, and different, it was set up exactly as my rooftop was with a few perks the old one didn't have. The lights, the hanging lamps, even the furniture, and our hammock were all the same. Set up identical, he'd added a stone and glass gas fireplace with a grilling station to the left of it, all against the wall. It was the same, right down to the fake grass carpet.

I stood stunned for a moment then, as I walked by mine and Rachel's chairs, I ran my hand across the seats Those chairs carried a lot of memories on them, and they'd know *way* too much if they could hear.

"See, I had the ass print chairs set up here for you guys."

"Thank you. Oh baby, thank you so much!" I jumped up, wrapping myself around him before kissing him slowly.

He brought me to the ground. The new fake grass was prickly and I knew it would hurt like the dickens later, but I didn't care. I was going to let him have his way with me again. This time though, I'd try to keep it down so not all of the Upper East Side would hear us. I let him set the pace. After all, he was the one who needed to recover from the last hour and Jesus Christ, I'm so glad I did.

Before Nathan, I used to laugh at women who'd say they could orgasm just from the passion of a kiss, and a touch in the right spot. I became one of those women the first night Nathan and I made love. He was my undoing, and he was taking me there again, nice and slow.

He kissed my neck, worked his way to my breasts as he slid his hand down the side of my body, and found me. My body responded before he even touched me. I arched my back pushing against his mouth as his fingers explored me. I slid my hand down his back, grabbed his ass, and pushed him against me.

He looked up with those blue eyes, smiled, and I was done. I didn't give a flying fuck if all five boroughs, and Hoboken, could hear me. He wrecked me. I whimpered a bit as I tried to get him in me but he pulled back, and grinned.

"No way, not on this. It'll be like razors on your skin. I'm pretty sure my knees are bleeding because my hands hurt like a motherfucker." He kissed my nose and stood up.

When he gave me his hand, I winced as he pulled me off the ground. He was right, that shit hurt. Neither of us was bleeding but goddamn it hurt.

He had everything set up for us over by the hammock. When I went to get in it, I noticed a leather covered journal type book sitting on the end table thingy.

"What's that?" I asked as he settled in next to me. It was a milder night, which allowed us to lay practically naked with our legs tangled with one another's and a light breeze blowing over us.

"*That* is something I've been waiting until we moved to share with you, but you've been such a hump-a-saurus lately I haven't had the chance to show you." He grinned and picked up the journal.

"A what? A hump-a-saurus? Seriously, that's a Rachelism. You did not come up with that on your own." I laughed and reached over to smack him in the arm.

"I assure you, I did." He laughed and handed me the book.

"Hey, it takes two to be hump-a-licious so I don't want to hear it. Plus, I never once heard you complain." I held the book above my face with one hand and ran my other hand over the leather cover.

"Don't drop that. It'll break your nose," he joked.

"I won't," I said and moved to open it.

"Nuh-uh. Not quite yet. Once you see what it is, I don't want you to feel obligated to indulge in it. Pick it up, put it down, read it together, talk about it, or don't talk about it. Whatever *you* choose, I'm okay with it." He let go of it.

"Nathan, I'm scared."

I tried to sit up but the hammock got sort of shaky so I laid back down.

"What is it?" My voice cracked a bit when I asked staring into those blue eyes that assured me I was the most loved woman in the world.

"It's my journal…from when I…it's my journal of everything that happened throughout my memory loss. From realizing I wasn't Lucas Black, right up to the night, I didn't know why but I had to find who was in that apartment because they were the missing piece. *You* were the missing piece, Jordan."

All I could hear was my heart pounding in my ears over my breathing as I watched his lips moving.

"This is everything. I want you know how I found you again."

For a long while, I lay there speechless.

Nathan broke the silence. "Jordan?"

He smiled as he searched my eyes.

Do I want to go down this rabbit hole? Of course, I do…but part of me doesn't because of the other women. He said he didn't have sex with them, but still…can I handle knowing about them?

"Jordie, say something. Please." He looked away.

I could see he was beginning to doubt the choice he made to show it to me, and I snapped out of it.

"I'm sorry. Yes, of course. I'm just having an

emotion overload." I chuckled. "I never asked you about any of this...and..."

"I know you didn't. This is me letting it all go." He kissed my forehead.

I opened it. On the inside cover, there was an inscription.

Finding Nathan.

Love, Mom and Dad

CHAPTER 8

It had to have been a good half hour we laid there in the hammock listening to the sounds of the city. Nathan was rocking us back and forth with his one foot hanging over the side. My head was on his chest. I held the leather-bound journal to my chest with my hand. If it weren't for him moving his foot, I'd have thought he was asleep. It wasn't an uncomfortable silence or anything. I think it was a mutual silence. I think I was mentally preparing to take it all in and he was mentally preparing to let it all out.

"Do you think I'll be able to handle this?" I asked him.

He stopped rocking us but didn't say anything at first. Finally, he said, "Do you think you'll be able to handle this?"

"I asked you first." I gave a tight-lipped smile with a non-enthusiastic chuckle.

"Shouldn't you be asking yourself that question, Jordan?" He sounded frustrated.

"Hey, don't be like that Nathan. I wasn't exactly

prepared for this."

He sighed really loud, and raked his fingers through his hair. "Babe, I wouldn't have given you it if I didn't think you could handle it. I don't think you fully understand how I see you. You are not just this smart, sexy, gorgeous, vixen that I would like to keep in bed all day, every day, might I add. You…you are the strongest person I have ever known. *Ever.* I mean, I had a pretty good idea you were one tough broad when I saw you take a hit like a champ. I'm still impressed by that shit, by the way." He gave a quick laugh then he turned his head to look at me. We were nose to nose.

"That's right, look at these guns," I joked and kissed my flexed bicep. He took my hand, leaving my other one still across my chest holding the journal.

"Not physically strong. You have balls of steel but you aren't very strong. Remember, I'm the one that held you back when you went after him." He chuckled. "I mean mentally strong. You had to have one hell of an ability to put mind over matter to get up after he clocked you. Jordan, he hit you like a man and you weren't going to let him get the best of you. *That* takes an incredibly strong person. I knew, at that very moment, you were different. You were the one that could handle all my baggage. All the craziness, fans, the paps. All of it. So yeah, I think you can handle *this.*"

"Jesus Christ, I asked a simple question. A yes or no would have sufficed." I laughed and handed him the journal. "Put this on the side table, please."

He took the journal, set it down, then he crinkled his eyebrows with a sadness.

I gave him my best reassuring smile. "I love you, and thank you. You'll do this with me, right? Like, if I have questions and stuff?"

"Yep. Anything you need."

"What if I get mad, or jealous, or whatever? Are you going to get mad at me and say I'm being ridiculous?"

"I counted on two of the three things but 'whatever' is a lot of ground to cover."

"Shut up. You know what I mean." I smiled awkwardly.

"I do, and I won't. I promise."

"Good, because I need some of *you right* now." I leaned in and kissed him.

He kissed me back and then rolled out of the hammock onto his knees.

"Damn this shit is rough on the skin," he said, I assumed in reference to the fake grass.

"Where are you going?" I pouted while I tried to level myself in the right position so I didn't fall out of the hammock.

He stood, and gave me a hand. Then he picked up the journal.

"I'm starving. Woman, go cook me something."

He laughed as I complained and bent over to over to scratch my foot. He wasn't kidding about this grass stuff.

"Cheese omelet?"

"Nah, just unwrap me a pop tart and call it a night." He winked.

"I think the pizza place is open until three on Friday nights. They stay open for the bar rush," I said, but quickly realized we didn't live near the pizzeria anymore.

"I'll take care of it," he said when we reached the door to go back inside.

Once we got back in the apartment, he grabbed his phone and disappeared into the other room. I picked up my phone. I had a few texts. One was from

Fiona—a picture of Nathan's dad in the recliner with Nate on his chest. Both of them out cold. Then there was another one from her of almost the identical picture except clearly it was a pic of an old photograph. The text that came with it said

> *Nearly 28 years ago. I hope you kids have a relaxing weekend. See you Sunday.*

The next text was from Rachel.

> *Tonight was fanfuckingtabulous please tell me we r gunna do that again soon. K? <3*

I smirked as I texted her back.

> *Do you know that Nathan said 'hump-o-saurus?! Stop teaching him words like that. LOL And yes, it was a blast and yes we'll do it again soon. <3*

> *Three pointer for the hot shot! I didn't teach him that LOL*

I woke up the next morning on my own. No alarm, no baby crying, no Emma needing to know where her hairbrush was. Nada. At first, I thought for sure I was dead. I was in a huge bedroom I hadn't fully acclimated to yet, there was a thin stream of light coming through the gigantic curtains, and just...silence.

Then the banging on the wall began and I knew all was well. One of Nathan's button down dress shirts was hanging over the chaise lounge by the window. *Yes, there's a fucking chaise lounge by my window. The floor to ceiling window.*

I picked up the shirt, slipped it over my head, and grabbed a pair of panties out of my drawer. When I started to make my way to what we refer to as the 'spare room,' the banging stopped and turned into a clanging of sorts.

"Whatcha' doin?" I poked my head in and saw Nathan was adjusting this bracket thingy on the wall.

"I…" he paused while he grunted adjusting the bars. "I am putting up the TV mount." He stopped and smiled.

"Well, it sounds like you're wreckin' the joint." I walked over to him.

"Wait, we only have the three TV's. What's this for?" I looked confused.

"I'm going to make this a media room, television with a camera and the whole set up. Right here is going to be a cutting booth, and over here–" He walked to the corner and extended his arms out as he described everything to me. "Here, will be the conference center where I can have meetings via video chat instead of having to fly off somewhere for a half a day meeting. Ya know?"

He was very animated and very excited.

"And there," he pointed up by the TV mount, "will be the green screen for when I need a touch up or have to reshoot something simple. I won't have to leave again for something miniscule. They can green screen whatever is needed. It's all very convenient and so much easier." He was beaming.

"I like the sound of all of that." I pulled him against me. "Will there be a big conference table in here?" I pointed behind me. "One I can hop up on and…sit…and watch you…work?" I said it slow and teasingly.

"Well, there will be now." He grabbed me by my behind and lifted me up so I could wrap my legs around him. "Oh woman, you and that messy hair in my shirt, wrapped around me. Are *you* trying to kill me now?" he joked.

I let my legs drop and hopped down. "That's not

funny. At all." I looked up at him.

"It was a joke, Jordan. If you and I can't make light of it, we'll never move past it."

"I thought giving me the journal was us moving past it?" I said, gathering my hair to one side, and shifting to lean on my other foot.

He stood and kissed my forehead. "Go get yourself some coffee and meet me back in bed." He winked and playfully shoved me off.

"I'm not in..." I started but he put his hand over my mouth to shush me.

"Just trust me. Get the coffee, oh and your glasses. We are going to read for a little bit before all the stuff gets here."

"The stuff, for in here, is being delivered today? When did you begin to plan all of this?" I stopped at the doorway and turned to him.

"Why do you think I wanted at least five bedrooms *and* an office?" He winked.

"Oh yeah, heh. It never clicked. But wait, if this is for that, what's the office for?" I must have had the most confused expression on my face because it made him bust out in a short laugh.

"I was thinking about seeing if it could be used for my assistant when I finally get to hiring one. Since it's in the front of the apartment, has a mini kitchen a wet bar, and a bathroom, nobody will have to go traipsing through the place," he said while he picked up the tools and put them in a toolbox I had no idea we even had.

"That's fine. As long as she isn't psycho, I'm cool with it. I'll see you in bed." I gave him a shy smile. I leaned back holding onto the doorjamb, and swung myself out to the hallway.

I was petrified. I just had to trust Nathan was right about me being strong enough. As much as I wanted to know, I didn't want to know.

I made it back to our bedroom before Nathan did. I arranged all the pillows so I'd be comfortable and ready. Then I got up and rearranged them again, got back in bed, then I was up one more time for what would be a quick pee, and another pillow arrangement. I was like the dog circling on the blanket and digging at it until it was just right. *Finally,* I settled back in and cleaned my glasses. I could hear Nathan coming down the hallway, finishing up a phone call, I guessed. Either that or he was discussing with himself delivery times.

"Yep, sounds good, man. See you around four." He tossed his phone on the chaise and dove onto the bed on top of me, destroying my perfect pillow arrangement.

"Nayy-ayayay-thannnn. I just got them right." I tried to skootch out from under him but he wasn't budging.

"Oh no, watch out, the pillow destructor is here to wreck your serious pillow business," he said in a mock monster voice, laughing. He let the full weight of his body come down on me, causing all the air to whoosh out of my lungs at once. I caught my breath and laughed with him.

"I'm serious, dammit! Do you know how many times I fixed those?" I wriggled under him.

"Three. Once, twice, got up to pee, then a third time, and now it'll be four, I'm assuming after I take advantage of you."

"No advantage taking right now. We are going to start this. Otherwise, Crasty McNasty here will keep on procrastinating." I pointed to myself.

"All right, I was just testing you anyhow. I would *never* take advantage of you." He had that shocked 'who-me?' expression and then rolled over so I was on top of him, and he was poking me.

"Oh, c'mon now. How do you expect me to allow a perfectly good hard-on go to waste?" I said as I rubbed up against him.

He grabbed my hips and began moving me back and forth. Who was I to complain?

"You sure you don't wanna work off some of that tension before we dive into this head first?" He actually bumped up on me when he said the word head.

"Sending subliminal messages, are we?" I nudged him back the best I could from my position.

"Why, is it working?" He grinned and pulled me down to him by the front of my shirt.

"I am the luckiest man in the world. And I'm not just saying that because you think I'd like a blow job or anything..." His smile turned into a shit-eating grin as I backed up so I could see what he was up to. "I say this only because you give the *best* blow jobs."

He busted out laughing and covered his face with his fore arms in defense because he knew what was coming.

"Oh my god," I shrieked as I grabbed the first pillow I could get my hands on and started to whack him with it. I'll admit my face felt like it had turned bright red.

He flipped me back over and pinned me down by my wrists.

"I mean it. I'm the luckiest man alive. I love you so much. So. Much." He loosened his grip, only to run his fingers down my arms and over my breasts, where he undid the first few buttons exposing me. He sucked in a deep breath as he took one of my breasts in his hand and bent down to kiss me.

I had no willpower when it came to him. Nathan, the pillow destructor, was the love of my life.

CHAPTER 9

July 3rd

I'm not sure what I'm supposed to say here because I'm not really sure of anything. This is what I do know, though.

My name is actually Nathan Harper, not Lucas Black as I had previously believed.

My parents brought me home from a hospital in NYC about a week ago. I was shot and from the looks of it beat within an inch of my life, and minus one spleen. That doesn't bother me as much as the bullet hole in my side thing I've got going on here.

I'm 27 soon to be 28.

I'm an actor and a popular one apparently.

My best friend's name is Tyler.

His girlfriend is sort of nuts. No, seriously, she looks at me like she is trying to penetrate my brain when she isn't giving me the stink eye. I wonder what the hell I did to her in the past.

So pretty much all I've got is I have a hell of a gash

on my head, I was definitely shot and nobody will tell me what the hell happened. They keep telling me that it's something I'd need to remember on my own. They can't put thoughts and ideas into my head. I have to figure out everything about 'The Incident' without being pushed to remember.

I can only remember bits and pieces of things.

I know my parents are my parents because I can see chunks of them in my mind. Tyler, same thing, bits and pieces that somehow fit in there. Being a celebrity is sort of hard to wrap my head around because I don't really remember much of that at all. I thought a character was real life there for a few days, so yeah. It's one I'm trying to get a handle on.

My mom suggested I watch a few of my movies, that perhaps it will shake things up a bit in my mind. I'd beg to differ...I think things are shaken up quite enough.

Above all, I can't lose this hollowness. I'm told its 'normal' and once it all starts coming back to me, it will fill in. For now, I need to work on it just like a puzzle. Put the edges together first then work on filling it in from there...one piece at a time.

I flipped the journal over, and placed it on my lap spine up and drummed my fingers on it for a few seconds. I turned to Nathan who was lying on his side, head propped up on his elbow pulling at a stem of a feather poking out of the down comforter.

"So?" He asked and looked up at me.

I could normally read his expressions easily but for the life of me, I couldn't figure out what was going through his head.

"Well, it's a lot like what I thought you were going through at the time. I think that's to be expected. No?" I questioned.

"What do you mean by it's a lot like what you thought I went through? What's different?" He sat up against the headboard and adjusted himself.

"Well, what I mean is, all of it was to be expected. The bits and pieces, the memories, the only thing that didn't cross my mind was you feeling hollow. I can totally understand that now, but then, not so much. I guess because the last words you said to me were, 'Now, I need my rest. If you aren't going to blow me, get out'."

"I said that?" His eyes almost popped out of the sockets.

"You, you don't remember the hospital? Like, at all?" I was shocked.

"Nope, the first thing I remember was a day or two after getting home from the hospital and we were staying at a hotel. I woke up, went into the living area and said "Hi, mom." And she busted out in tears. I didn't know what the fuck was going on but I for sure wasn't about to start asking questions at that point. After a few sobs, she walked over and hugged me a bit too tight. I winced and she apologized then asked me my name. With that, I was positive she'd lost her mind so I said it slowly, 'Nathan.' She hugged me again gently and sobbed silently. She just kept saying, 'that's right...your name is Nathan.' And from that day forward I started putting the pieces together."

"What was it like when something would come back to you? Was it like you had to work to make sense of it or did you know what it was immediately?"

"It was both. For instance, take my mom and dad. Right away, I knew who they were as soon as it came back to me. It wasn't like it was a thought in my mind, *then* I said out loud, 'ohhh hey, yeah, I remember you.' It was more like I went to bed not knowing but woke up and it just came out of my mouth. A lot of things were like that." He explained.

"Heh." I responded as I stared off at the wall.

I had so many questions rattling through my head for so long and now that he's answering them, I questioned again if I really wanted to know or not. Maybe he sensed that because he took the journal off my lap and closed it up.

"Perhaps later on, or tomorrow, we can cover some more ground with this because, honestly, the only thing I want to cover right now is you." He tugged on my shirt and that got my attention. He smacked his thighs and gave me that lopsided grin he knew I couldn't resist.

After our neked morning romp around, we decided to shower, get dressed and venture out into the world after all, for some coffee. Luck had it there was a Starbucks right across the street from the apartment. We couldn't go too far anyhow because the delivery people would be there in a few hours.

I was sort of excited to see what that room would look like finished. It would take a week or two to get everything built and assembled. In the meantime, we needed to find Nathan an assistant. I certainly couldn't do it, nor did I want to. Fuck that job. Don't shit where you eat, ya know?

"Good Morning Jordie. Nate," Ryan, the barista, greeted us as he wrote our names on the cups.

Usually he'd write a little message or note on the side along with it. After they made our usual order, he handed me mine. I turned the cup to see what he wrote. It read, 'Keep smiling' with a little heart next to it followed by 'You go Glenn CoCo'. I immediately busted out at the *Mean Girls* reference and he winked at me.

What really made me almost lose my bladder was

when Nathan read his cup, "And none for Gretchen Weiners." I lost my shit completely. Nathan was somewhat amused not nearly as much as me though. Nathan grumbled something when he held the door open for me as we left.

"What's wrong? *That* was hilarious." I said still smiling.

"Maybe to you, because you don't see that the kid is infatuated with you." He said taking a sip of his steaming hot coffee. I mean it was really steaming. "Look, he's even trying to scald me." He took the lid off and raised his cup a little. "Imagine, I survived the insane ex-husband but death by Coffee house Ryan is what did me in."

We both laughed.

"Speaking of surviving. I was thinking we should totally come up with a code word. I mean had Rach and I not did the 'Holler' thing I doubt if Frank would have caught on. So we need one." I said before taking a sip of my latte'. That was at the perfect temperature might I add.

"Oh, like a safe word?" His eyes lit up like the Griswold's house at Christmas time.

"No, you perv." I joked. "Like a code word that the entire family can use in case any of us need help but can't-ask type deal." I explained.

"I think we've reached our quota on dangerous situations for one lifetime, but I guess you never know what else could come out from the crazy closet you have." He teased.

"I hate you." I laughed.

"Love you too." He said with a chuckle.

"Pick a word." I said as we crossed the street and I had to pick up the pace because I didn't see a cab rounding the corner at Mach nine. When we reached the sidewalk across the street we stopped.

"Flapjack." Nathan said.

"You're hungry?" I asked confused.

"No, the code word for daaangerrr." He exaggerated and we began walking again.

" Ohhhh." I snorted.

"Flapjack it is then." I agreed.

As we approached our building, the doorman stopped us to give Nathan an envelope left for him. Nathan's agent dropped off a list of assistants in the city that he considered the best. Pfttt…for the salary they were getting they better be the best and then some.

"Why would he drop it off here? Ever hear of email?" I questioned as I took my sweater off and threw it on the chair. The first week we lived here, I'd open the door and immediately throw my keys to the right where the table used to be in the old place. I'm finally getting used to not having one there.

"You know Stanley, nosey bastard. He probably wanted to scope out the new place." Nathan said as his phone went off. He pulled it out to check it and chuckled.

"Speakin' of Stan. I just got an eeeemmaaailll from him." He jiggled his phone in my face.

"Look at that he does know how to use it after all." I plopped down on the couch and picked up my coffee for a sip as Nathan read the email.

"He wanted to give me the name of another available assistant that just crossed his desk. Apparently, she's the best and I should get her in for an interview before someone else snatches her up. Evelyn Martinez."

"Good stuff, maybe you should call her now, try and set something up." I took another sip and chuckled when I looked at my cup. "Damn that kid cracks me up and wait. He is not infatuated with me FYI." I added.

He was about to comment but the phone rang.

"Saved by the bell," I mumbled.

It was the concierge calling to let us know the delivery guys had arrived and wondered if he should send them up. After he hung up, he handed me the envelope and asked me to take down Evelyn's number to set something up for him to meet with her...ASAP.

"Hey, I'm going to do this down at *my* office," I said to him after I put the number in the envelope.

"When do you want to meet with her?" I asked.

"I figured you'd do it." He made his way to go open the door.

"Me? Why me? She's gunna' be your assistant." I scrunched my face up confused.

"Jordie, let's be honest here...if you don't like her it's not happening anyhow so we may as well skip the middle man." He chuckled as drank his now non-boiling coffee.

He had a point.

"Oki doki." I grabbed my purse and stretched up on my tippy toes to give him a kiss. He smacked my ass as I walked out the door. I let out a yelp just as the elevator dinged and opened up.

"Do you want me to get Frank to take you?"

"Nah, I'll take cab, and then see if he's around to drive me back," I answered just as Frank was getting out of the elevator.

"Where am I taking you?" He asked as he stepped back to allow the two men with a ginormous box out of the elevator.

"Oh, never mind then. I'll take the truck." I smiled and moved out of the way.

* * *

"Straight through, and then to the left down the hall with that, guys. The second room on the right." Nathan instructed the men.

"Okay, keep me posted." Nathan said before he walked off after the men.

"Watch the walls dude," was the last thing I heard him say before he turned the corner.

"What's up Frank? Everything okay?" I dug my keys out of my purse.

"Everything's fine. The doorman called to let me know there was quite a few men with a lot of boxes wanting to deliver them up here, so he wanted to check with me first."

"What, did you want to make sure Jason wasn't delivering little men in boxes to kill us?" I snorted.

"Nope, just doing my job, Mrs. Harper," he said dryly.

I snapped my head up immediately.

"Seriously?" I stared at him blankly.

He winked at me and I shoved his shoulder. "You're such a dick sometimes!"

"Where you headed?"

"The bar. I have to start setting up interviews to find Nathan a new assistant," I said as I pulled my keys out.

"You want me to drive you over?"

"Nope, I'm good. Thanks." I pressed the down button.

CHAPTER 10

When I pulled up in front of the bar, I was tempted to go up in the old place. I didn't though because I really had no reason to. Since we moved, Frank had been back there a few times to check up on things. He had some belongings stored from when he lived there so he'd report all was well. He went back to living at a hotel a block away from us because it was too far from the new place in case he had to get to us fast.

I unlocked the door to the bar, and yanked it open. It seemed so much heavier now that I wasn't there as much. I walked in, flipped on some lights, tossed my crap on the bar, and made my way to my office with the envelope. It didn't even feel like *my* office any longer. Rachel had turned that shit into her own personal girl cave. Everything was new, right down to the flooring. It needed a makeover but I sure did miss my squeaky chair.

I plopped in the seat, pulled the number out of the envelope and dialed Ms. Martinez's phone number from my cell. Someone answered on the third ring.

"This is Evelyn speaking."

"Hi, Evelyn. I'm calling on the behalf of Nate Harper. He's looking to hire a new PA and your name came highly recommended. Would you be interested in meeting with me for an interview?"

She was silent.

"Hello?" I hated silence on the other end of telephone calls.

"Yes. You said Nate Harper?"

"I did. Is this a position you may be interested in interviewing for?" I asked the question again because at this point, she seemed dumber than a bag Courtney Stoddens, and slow as balls. However slow balls may be...I never quite understood that expression but...whatever...she was slow.

"It is," she replied.

Holy shitballs...this is like pulling teeth in the 16th century.

"Great, I have tomorrow at 2:00 P.M..."

"How about today? Say, in about an hour?" She interrupted me.

"Today? Sure, I guess I can try to rearrange a few things. I have someone waiting right now, so an hour should be fine," I lied. I didn't want her to think she was our first call just because she came highly recommended. "Are you familiar with the East Village at all?"

"Yes, what's the address?" She asked. This chick was all business, not a hint of reaction or emotion in her voice.

"The Post on East 13th street. When you're about to arrive please give me a call on this number, and I'll come let you in," I instructed her.

"Will do. See you shortly. Thank you." *Click.*

My phone beeped three times at the disconnect.

Bitch just hung up on me?

Heh. I might like her after all.

I heard the door unlock and some light stream in. My hand immediately went under my desk for the gun.

Damn girl, those instincts really kicked in. Like a ninja.

I felt around for it and remembered Rachel had replaced the gun for some mace and a Taser gun instead. They'd confiscated both of mine after the whole incident. I'm lucky that's all they did. It's not like they were registered to me or anything. They were Jason's guns.

It was obvious it was somebody I knew because they had a key but still, once I heard the familiar clickity clack followed by the 'Hellooo bitch, don't mace me', I relaxed.

"Hey. What are you doing here so early?" I asked her as she threw her stuff on the chair in the corner.

"I have to catch up on a few things. I've been busy with Tyler's gigs and shit. What are you doing here with clothes on? Aren't the kids gone for the weekend? I figured your Hills would be Alive with the Sound of...."

"Ok, enough. Ha ha, you're a riot." I adjusted myself in the chair laughing.

"For reals, I didn't expect to see you. What's up?"

"Nathan is having his home office slash board room slash sound booth slash green screen set up today. I came down here to set up some interviews for a new PA for him. Lila's last week *was* last week. So she's working her new job and Nathan."

"Good luck with that." Rachel reached across me and shuffled through some papers.

"Can I help you with something?" It was a rhetorical question. She knew I hated that shit.

"Yeah, you can get out of my chair so I can get this done and still make it to Tyler's gig then be back here by 9:00." She didn't miss a shuffling beat, just kept on.

"Your chair?" My facial expression read 'holy shit you have BO' but my mind was saying 'bitch what?'

"Yes, my chair. Your chair is over there in the corner laid to rest. Now please, just let me get this done and I'll be out of your way." She huffed as she grabbed a folder off the filing cabinet and turned to me.

"Fine with me. I have someone coming in about an hour for an interview. May I conduct business in my office then, boss?" I pushed way from the desk allowing myself to roll back freely with my arms and legs extended straight out in front of me before I stood and moved out of her way.

"Holy shit, don't fucking start Jordan. I don't give a shit what you do after I'm finished." She plopped in the chair, exhaled loudly, and put her head down.

"Rach, are you okay?" I moved my head so I could see her face but she'd buried it in her hands by then.

"I'm fine Jords. I'm sorry. I'm just stressed."

"What can I do to help? Is it too much here? I can hire a full time office person, Rachel. I didn't mean to keep this on you for so long. I thought I'd be back by…"

"No, it's not too much." She snapped, "I just…I'm fine."

I could have been hallucinating but I think I saw tears in her eyes.

"Oh for the love of all that is Holy, Rachel, look at me dammit," I yelled.

"WHAT? Fine, I think Tyler is cheating on me! Happy? Now *please,* let me get this shit done." She quickly clammed up again.

"I'm sure he isn't..." I began, but then thought better of it.

I knew she'd talk when she was ready, but I intended to grill Nathan when I got home.

"And keep your big fat mouth shut. *Do not* say anything to Nathan." She didn't look up at me.

"Got it." *My ass, don't say anything.* "Rach, I love you. I'm..."

"Don't apologize for something you had nothing to do with. Love you, too."

I walked out and closed the door to give her some space. She didn't need a lecture or a bitch venting sesh, she needed to sort out and compartmentalize everything, and digest it, *then* she'd be ready.

About fifteen minutes later, I received a call from Evelyn.

"I'm outside, Mrs. Harper," she simply said.

I looked at the time. She was twenty minutes early.

"Oh, ok, you're early. I'll be right there."

"If you aren't fifteen minutes early, you're late," she said in her flat monotone voice. *All business. I like that.*

I wish I'd had a camera to catch the expression on my face when I opened the door. I'd imagine it was like the Titanic. One second above water, the next a sinking ship. My smile took a nosedive when I saw exactly who Evelyn Martinez was. Bristol Santana's old assistant. *Oh. Hell. No.*

"Ms. Martinez? I wasn't expecting..."

"Expecting what? I need a job and Mr. Harper needs a personal assistant. It really isn't *that* unexpected now, is it?" She smiled.

I had to give it to her, she not only had a point, I mean, we were told she'd just become available, but she had a gorgeous smile, too.

"Well, come in. My office is occupied at the moment so I hope you don't mind doing this at the bar," I said as I walked towards it.

"Not at all."

Before Bristol, she had worked for a few big names. All of them had left amazing references for her. I went through all her paperwork and I think I asked all the right questions. She was perfect for the job, more than punctual, efficient, works well under pressure, and had worked with huge talent on some important projects along with it. But, could I trust her to do the same with Nathan? I mean, I did get her fired in the first place.

"Well, that about does it. I have a few more interviews and then I'll go over everything with Nathan, but we'll let you know either way." I smiled as I straightened out the papers making sure I didn't make eye contact with her.

"Other interviews? Let's see, there's Misty Rivers who is looking for a position," she began.

"Misty Rivers? Sounds like a porn name." I snorted. "I assure you, her name precedes her." She cracked a grin that told me she was serious.

"Then there's Ross Simon. Organized, efficient, professional, but he brings his personal life into the work place and when that happens, it isn't pretty. Oh, and of course, there's my favorite candidate, Sophie McBride. She is a name-dropping swag whore. She has no shame walking down 5th Avenue letting all the stores know who she's 'shopping for', and then they hand over the free shit to give to you that you'll never see. There are good reasons they need a job." She snickered.

"There's a reason you need a job," I quipped.

"Yeah, *you*. You're the reason I need a job."

"Hold the fuck up. I don't know who you think you

are exactly coming into my establishment *again,* and being a raging bitch, but I don't think so. There's the door." I pointed to it.

"It's your choice. I don't mix business with personal." She took her bag off the bar and put it over her shoulder.

"Yeah, just like you didn't the night you got canned?"

"That." She paused. "*That* was different, which ironically, brings me to my last bit of advice. Watch out for Bristol. She *will* do whatever it takes to get what she wants, even if it means breaking a few hearts and marriages to get it." She turned and walked towards the door.

"What does that even mean?" I asked her.

"Hopefully, you'll never have to find out." She pushed the door open and walked out leaving me standing there dumbfounded.

"Bitch," I muttered, and took the list out of the envelope to start making calls.

After I called Ms. Rivers, Mr. Simon, and Ms. McBride to set up interviews, I could feel it in my gut that Evelyn was right. But, at least I'd know by the end of the day if we had an assistant or not. Luckily, those three had nothing going on so they were available to meet with me that same day.

When I heard Rachel yelling from inside my office, I rushed in there. Poor fool on the other end of that call must have done something serious to piss her off.

"And don't fucking call back here because we don't know how to read, write, or tell time in this place, so you can keep your crappy books, clocks and commemorative dinner plates." She slammed the phone down.

Yeah, Nathan and I were going to have a chat.

* * *

After my interview with Misty Rivers, I wondered if I should have just cancelled the other two because I suspected Evelyn was definitely right. Who showed up to a job interview in eight-inch fuck me boots with a skirt that was two inches from her kuka? Misty Rivers did, that's who. She was a definite no for the job.

I had a few minutes until Mr. Simon arrived so I trolled my normal gossip sites, got my fix, and against my better judgment went to Nate Nation. I wished I hadn't because as soon as I opened the first thread, I saw that BratelsReal was at it again. First of all, what kind of internet name is BratelsReal? Really? Couldn't come up with something a bit more creative?

I scrolled down to the first post and glanced through it. Same ol' same ol', I was a bitch, Nathan and Bristol belonged together, and our marriage was a sham.

Whatever you say there BratelsReal. You need to get your ass off the internet and start worrying about your own life instead of mine and while you're getting that taste of reality seek a head doctor because you need some serious professional help.

I was reminded once again as to why I stayed off that site since discovering it.

Mr. Simon had called to let me know he was outside. He was very tall and sort of lanky. He had on a white bowtie with a pink and white checkered button down shirt tucked into his khakis. He had on black thick-rimmed glasses and had a man purse like Frank. Okay, what was it with bowties and glasses? I mean didn't the fashion industry think people looked challenged enough with the skinny jean thing? You know every last one of those designers was sitting back and laughing all the way to the bank. 'Look at that man in tights, hey let's get him in a bowtie and some glasses to perfect the ensemble...' Just no, okay? No.

While I was interviewing Mr. Simon, his phone must have vibrated twenty times. At one point, he pulled it out to turn it on completely silent, but I was annoyed by then.

"Sorry, having some family issues. I thought I had it on silent." He looked at the phone, studied it for a second then gasped. "Oh, you are such a bitch."

He said those words out loud. When realized what he was doing, he shoved the phone back in his pocket. "Seriously, I'm so sorry."

"I'm not interested in apologies, **Mr.** Simon. Thank you, you can show yourself out." I stood from my chair and motioned towards the door with my hand.

"But you haven't even seen my ref..."

"I've seen enough, thank you. You first." My hand was still waving in the direction of the door.

He knew I wasn't playing after that and picked up his murse, and sulked out through the bar to the door.

"Thank you for taking the time to come down but I don't think it's a good fit. Take care, Mr. Simon." I walked away as the door closed.

At that point, I knew I shouldn't even bother to interview Ms. McBride. Evelyn was now two for two. It didn't take a genius to see she'd be three for three. She wasn't bad mouthing people so much as she was actually trying not to waste my time. Heh, maybe the big, bad bitch wasn't so bad after all. I guess we'd find out.

I was about to pull my phone out of my pocket when Sophie McBride walked in. She caught the door as the last shmoe left. She was polite and impeccably dressed. Right down to her nine hundred dollar Louboutins. Oh, and when I said her Gucci bag was gorgeous, she told me that it was a gift from her last employer. *I bet it was.*

When I got back to the apartment, there was still a shit ton of people there. I heard a lot of power tools and men talking over them. I poked my head in the room to look for Nathan. I didn't see him in there but when I turned around he was standing behind me. I jumped and let out a squeal, which made Nathan laugh.

"What the hell, Nathan? You scared me. You're lucky I didn't go all kung-pow on your ass," I said, and it just made him laugh harder.

"Yeah, kung-pow alright. Kung Pao chicken is about all you'll go." He grinned and gave me a kiss. "So, get some interviews set up?"

"I did. Actually, I got them all done today. There's good news and there's bad news. Pick which one you want first," I said smacking the envelope on his arm.

"Surprise me."

"I got the newly available kick ass assistant." I grinned.

"Babe, that is awesome. Thank you so much. So what could possibly be so bad about that?" He crinkled his brows in confusion.

"Well, she's Bristol's recently let go assistant." I began to walk away back down the hallway towards the living room.

"What? No, Jordan. I can't hire her. That's just...tacky. No way." He put the drill down he was holding and followed me.

"Alright fine, here's your other choices. There's Ms. Misty Rivers who showed up in fuck me boots and a headband for a skirt. Then there's the Drama King himself, Ross Simon, or Sophie McBride, who's a 'Name dropping Swag Whore'. Then there's Evelyn, who is impeccably dressed, incredibly efficient and professional. So you get to pick between the drama king and swag whore..." I spun around and pointed at him.

"Wait, what about the other one, 'Misty'?" His voice deepened into a mock sultry tone as he pulled me towards him and laughed.

I slapped his arm and buried my face in his chest then looked up at him with a smile.

"Funny. Seriously, it wasn't even remotely pretty to look at. Besides, she was wearing some knock off of my black eight inch Chanel thigh highs. You've been there already." I laughed.

"And done that," he replied just as a huge thud, crash, and a few "shits" were heard from the media room.

"To be continued..." He rolled his eyes and kissed my nose.

"I'll call Evelyn." I let go of his hands and grinned.

"I figured as much." He shook his head and chuckled as he walked back towards the room.

CHAPTER 11

July 8th

Today would be one of those days that I'd say 'I lost my mind', but unfortunately for me...that's what happened.

It started out with waking from a dream that I couldn't remember. Heh, imagine that, but at the same time I couldn't forget it. There was something, in the dream, that had my brain cranking in overdrive.

I finally got my stitches taken out. Dad wanted to pull them out himself and rub some dirt on it as the old saying goes, but Mom called him an idiot and had Frank take us to the Dr.'s. My parents are quite the comical duo, I know that much. I hope I can have that someday.

Frank is a pretty interesting guy. He definitely knows more about me than I do. I wondered if he could give me some info but when I asked him, he hesitated like he wanted to tell me and then he just shook his head and said someday kid, someday. While waiting in the Dr's office, a woman approached me for an autograph. She handed me a piece of paper with her number and 'coffee one day?' written on it. Mom was practically stabbing this chick in the face with her dagger eyes, and after she walked away went on about how trashy it was to throw herself at a man like that, especially in front of his mother. Then, like she does, she said...give my brain some time to try and process and digest.

I just wanted out of this fucking hotel room and have a conversation with someone other than Mom, Dad, Tyler or Frank. So, I called her.

We met up in the downstairs restaurant of the hotel. I thought I could actually hear what the girl was saying instead of being disrupted every five minutes or the paparazzi clicking away. Of course, Frank stood guard at the entrance. I saw him stop her as she got to the front. They spoke for a minute. Her name is Charlie, short for Charlene. She's 24 years old and works at Hooters. I like Hooters' hot wings...and that's about all we had in common. She did eventually ask how I was feeling. I tried to play it off like I knew what had happened so I didn't seem like I was a complete vegetable. She stopped talking after that. I walked her out, and thanked her for the company and kissed her on the cheek. Instantly, I felt like someone ripped my insides out and gutted me.

I haven't been able to shake that feeling yet. I know my brain has more holes than the Moonlight Bunny Ranch but this one...this one...this one is important. I need to find out what it's all about before I go mad.

I closed Nathan's journal and put it on my nightstand. I laid my head on Nathan's chest and just listened to him breathe for a few minutes before I ran my finger up and down his stomach.

"Any questions?" He asked as he took in a sharp breath, I'm guessing due to the close proximity of my fingers to the waistband of his boxers.

"Yes," I said flatly, and slipped my hand into his boxers.

I wasn't exactly sure why I did it, because it was really out of character for me. We both knew it. We were the spur of the moment couple. Something funny, playful, or passionate always led us to our sexy time but I wasn't really sure what I was feeling. The only thing I knew at that moment was I needed to feel how much he loved me. I mean, I could *see* how much but I suddenly felt an insecurity I've never had before. I think it was the realization that at one point Nathan really had no idea we existed. I seriously began to question if I'd be able to handle the whole journal thing. Nothing had even happened yet and my insides are already twisting.

I sat up on my knees and positioned myself between his legs. I could tell he was confused as I pulled his boxers down in the front and bent so my mouth hovered over him.

"Jordan, what are you..." he began but before he could finish his sentence, I silently answered his question. He let out a strained hiss of pleasure and put his hand in my hair. It was what he always did when I went down on him, but this time he guided my head up.

"Jordie, what's going on?" His blue eyes searched mine as he held my head up and rubbed it at the same time.

"Is this a problem?" I forced a grin.

"As far as theory works, I'd say hell no...but as far as how you and I work, yes, it's a problem. Come up here." He pulled me up.

I yanked on my shirt to take it off but he stopped me. That did not help with my issue. I wanted to scream in the worst way. I pushed his hand away and took my shirt off anyway.

"Let's talk about what's going on in there." He tapped my forehead lightly.

"You said if I didn't want to talk, it was okay. You said, however I wanted to work through it, you would with me." I stared down at his chest while I spoke.

"I did…you're right. Just do me one small favor, please?" He bumped his hips underneath me and I smiled because I knew he still wanted me.

"I'll try." I gave him a sarcastic grin.

"Can you tell me why this is how you want to work through it?" He ran his hands up and down my thighs as I sat there still straddling him.

Why? Why do I want to handle it like this? Because I'm captain crazy pants that's why…somewhere in my brain I fried a circuit because I know you love me…again…now…but there was a time you didn't, and I don't know if I can deal with that.

"I just wanna' be close to you," I whispered close to his ear.

"That's good enough for me."

He gripped my hips hard and pulled me as close as possible against him. Somehow, in one quick motion, he was on his knees and on top of me.

My heart was pounding. For a split second, I felt like I was being judged on a high dive or some shit. Like my performance mattered. *What the hell is wrong with me? This is the one person who knows me as well as I know me. He loves me…crazy pants and all.*

The moment I locked eyes with Nathan, I snapped out of it. He found the spot on my neck that drove me nuts and my hands found his hair. Now I was a definite foreplay kind of girl but tonight I really needed it to be quick and dirty. He knew all of my little quirks that let him know I was ready but when his hand slipped in my panties, he stopped for a second, took in a deep breath while he removed them, and exhaled something incoherent but none the less it made me nuts. I reached down, moved his hand with mine as he bit down on my shoulder.

"Baby, I won't last five minutes if you keep this up," he said into my mouth as he kissed me.

"Why not?" I teased him by pushing his fingers down further. I needed to hear it, feel it. I needed to reassure myself, however fucking asinine it was. I needed it.

"Oh my god woman, seriously…holy fuck, you're gorgeous and you're all mine." He sat up on his knees between my legs, pushing his fingers deeper into me.

When I arched upward, he replaced his hand with mine, ran his wet fingers up my stomach, and palmed my breast as he watched me. His eyes followed every move my hand made. The more into it I got, the rougher he got. The louder I got, the more he told me how much he couldn't wait to get in me. His expression said it all, not his words, his expression.

I closed my eyes and I could feel how much he loved me. When I opened them and saw he was pleasuring himself at the same time, it sent me over the edge…that was my undoing. I hadn't even fully finished before I felt his full weight on me and then he was inside. His arms wrapped under my back so his hands gripped my shoulders. He pulled me down to meet each of his thrusts. We were as close as possible and he'd got so deep that the aftershock came on fast and hard. I don't think I've ever had an orgasm like that before…I swear I saw colors. No shit. Colors. I may have even heard fireworks and the Star Spangled Banner, or it may have just been Nathan because I could hear him over my screams of pleasure.

* * *

It was early Sunday morning when my text alert went off, Nathan was still asleep so I grabbed my phone and headed to the kitchen. After I put on a pot of coffee...*yes, I am aware I'm the only person on the planet that doesn't use one of those k-kup single serving coffee machines FYI*...I checked my texts.

Please call me when you get a moment

"Even the good Father rested on Sunday...but not Evelyn Martinez." I snickered as I tapped her contact info.

"This is Evelyn." She answered on the first ring.

"Hey Evelyn, I just got your text. What's up?"

"Good morning Mrs. Harper. I'm sorry to bother you on the weekend but I had a few questions about tomorrow. Is now a good time?"

This woman was all business, and meant business. I was starting to doubt it was even the same bitch from the bar on Friday night.

"Please, call me Jordie, and sure, now is good."

She had some basic questions like what attire was required, what airlines Nathan preferred and in order of preference, was she salary or hourly and if she would be working as a mobile office or have a stationary one. Things like that and we never discussed an actual schedule so we got that out of the way as well.

"Nine AM sound good to you?" I propped the phone between my shoulder and ear as I poured myself another cup of coffee.

"Actually, would eight thirty be a problem? I drop my daughter off at school at eight, and I can hop on the 5 or 6 train from Grand Central to East 77th and the walk from there, on an average day, is seven minutes." She made the request in one long sentence.

"Sounds like you mapped this out pretty well. Sure,

eight thirty is fine." I laughed and took a sip.

"Yes, my daughter and I did a trial run early this morning so I could plan ahead," she replied.

All right, this was definitely a completely different woman from the other night. This was going to work out great.

"Well, that's about it then. See you at eight thirty. We can go over everything else tomorrow," I said as I sat at the table and opened my laptop.

"Thank you Jordie, for the opportunity. I know we didn't get off to a good start, and I apologize for that." She sounded sincere, and well, who am I to hold a grudge? We all allow our bitchiness take over at one time or another.

"Thank you but an apology isn't necessary. We all have our moments." I laughed.

Shit, I was having my moment when I busted between Bristol and Nathan during their little photo op at the bar Friday night.

"See you in the AM. Take care," she said.

"See ya tomorrow." I hit the end button.

I sent Rachel a text to see how she was doing, checked my email, and then made my usual gossip rounds. Ugh, pictures from Friday night. Bristol and Nathan, AKA Brate. What a dumb fucking name. *Who does that? Oh, this is a cute one of Nathan and some woman. She's tiny, damn.*

The next one I saw made me laugh as much as it irked me. It was the pic of Nathan and Bristol that I busted into, so it looked as if Nathan was looking down Bristol's shirt whereas, he was really looking down at me. Fucking tabloids, they're always causing trouble.

Next stop on the crazy train was Nate-Nation. Well, Deloony was at it again. Her name was Delena but I nick named her Deloony and Delusional. Seriously, the bitch was both. I swear this chick had no life. She stayed online day, and night, it seemed like putting Bristol's head on my body or someone else's body. She even made these weird manipulations of them in bed together or some kind of bondage shit. It seriously creeped me out more than anything that someone had invested *this* much time into a relationship that, first of all, wasn't even real but also she didn't know any of us.

As I scrolled through Deloony-Land, I noticed one of the pics from the bar Friday night. It was captioned 'Nate sneaking a peak at his woman's goods'. *Ew…What. The. Fuck. For reals, this trick was straight up crazy.*

I slammed the laptop shut and started to make breakfast. I mumbled the entire time to myself about how he was *my husband* and how dare this stupid ass bitch go on a public place like that and say all that shit. I mean, wasn't there a law or something against doing that shit? Like slander or defamation of character? Something? *Anything?* I guess I was banging shit around, too, because I woke Nathan.

"What the hell is going on in here? I thought our kitchen was being ransacked. What's with all the racket, babe?" Nathan shuffled in all sleepy eyed and shirtless followed by a yawn.

"Holy shit, you scared me." I jumped back and almost knocked the bottle of OJ on the floor.

"I made you breakfast." I held up a plate of bacon and eggs with some toast and handed it to him.

"Okay, I forgive you." He gave me a dopey grin and a quick kiss.

I got him some coffee while he went to sit down at the table. When I set the cup down, he thanked me and chuckled.

"You didn't wake me up anyhow. My mom called.

They'll be here about six. They're heading over to Jersey to pick up Emma," he said with his mouth full.

"Okay," I answered.

"So, this is what's got you all cranky." He pointed to my laptop.

"No, I had to email Rachel because she didn't answer my text...and speaking of...she was a fucking nightmare at the bar yesterday when I saw her. Has Tyler said anything to you about them having problems because she's convinced he is stepping out on her?" I took a sip of my coffee and waited for him to finish chewing.

"What? Tyler, cheat? That is so ridiculous its borderline amusing," he said, then ate the last of his bacon.

"Well, she was bitching at me, and then went off on how he is being secretive and Amber seeing him over at the Starbucks in the Manhattan Mall with some blonde woman. Amber couldn't see what they were doing because they were sitting next to one another with their backs turned to the glass, but she managed to get a glimpse of him when she went in for a coffee. Like I said, though she couldn't see what they were doing, whatever it was, they were in their own little world. She even told Rach that he held the woman's hand up and was doing something to her fingers. That they were laughing really loud, but like they were in their own bubble. Nathan, she is devastated. Can you talk to him please, maybe poke around a bit, and see if you can find anything out?" I managed to get it all out to Nathan in one big breath.

"Are ya' done?" He asked as he stood up. "With your plate, that is."

He grinned.

"Yes, smartass I am. What do you know?" I stood up and followed him to the sink after he took my plate.

"I know nothing, Jordan. Naaahhh-thiiiing I say."
He put the plates in the sink and turned to me.

"Bullshit, you shitty liar that lies. You're lying! Tell
me or I will just assume the worst and go over there
rip his arms off and beat him with them."

He put his arms around my waist and kissed me.
"It's nothing bad, I promise. He isn't cheating on
her…"

"But she said he has been doing like triple amount
of gigs that he normally does and is never home.
That's why she drives herself nuts to make it to all of
his shows because he is always working now…or out
fondling blonde haired women's hands." I cut him off
mid-sentence.

"The two of you conjure up the most elaborate shit
ever. You should be writing dramedies, I swear." He
poked my side with his pointed finger then pushed off
the counter and walked past me to get more coffee.

"Don't change the subject bucko. What is going
on?" I demanded an answer this time.

"Jesus Christ, chill woman. You can't say anything.
It's a surprise. You promise?" He turned to me taking
a sip of his freshly poured cup of joe.

"Holy crap, Nathan, I *promise*. Now tell me." I
urged and whined.

"He's going to ask her to marry him. That woman
was the jeweler's assistant. The extra gigs have been
to pay for the ring. I offered to help him out but
nope…he said he had to earn it. He wanted her to see
how much he loves her by how hard he worked to get
to where he wants to be with her. Married."

I stood there in shock. Rachel…married? That was
something I never thought I'd see. Wow. Rachel
married.

"Thank god. Well I hope he doesn't wait too much

longer to ask because it's killing her inside. She's really hurt."

"He planned on doing it next weekend. His mom, brother, and sister are flying in for it," he said.

"Well damn. I hope she says yes." I laughed.

CHAPTER 12

Nathan's mom called at six o'clock to let us know that they were on their way back from Jersey and asked if she needed to pick anything up for dinner. After I hung up with her, I was lying on my stomach next to Nathan, eye level with his journal. I knew he saw me staring at it. I could feel his eyes on my back.

"Do you want to read a little more before we get up?" He asked me.

"No, I don't feel like moving right now."

"Well we have to." Nathan smacked me on the ass before he got out of bed.

I stayed in bed and watched him as he put on his boxers. Jesus Christ, he was a fine specimen. He tossed me my shirt and asked if I was sure.

"Yes, I'm sure I've had enough for one day. Besides, your parents and kids will be back soon. We don't need a repeat of what happened last time." I laughed as I sat up and tossed my shirt on to the chaise.

He leaned down and kissed me.

"It'll be fine, don't worry about it. I told you we'd do

this together," he said.

"That's just it, I don't know if I can read this with you. I mean, nothing has even happened yet and look how I freaked. All I could think about was sex, sex, sex, like that was the only way to hold onto you right then. How ridiculous is that?" I asked as I approached him. "And what's with the boxers? We need a shower." I wiggled my eyebrows at him.

He gave me my smile and dropped his shorts.

"I won't argue with that." He grabbed me around the waist and pulled me in tight.

By the time we got done showering, everyone was back. I hurried to get dressed to see my babies. I missed the shit out of them. It was nice to have me time with Nathan, and time to go to the bar, but I wanted to see my kids in the absolute worst way.

"Where are my beautiful babies?" I called out as I came down the hallway.

"I have the little one right here for you." Fiona handed Nate to me.

"Look at you. I've missed my baby boy." I baby talked to my son and gave him a kiss.

"Where's Emma?" I looked around.

"I'm down here, Mom." I heard her shout from her room.

"Hi, Mom." Nathan gave Fiona a kiss on the cheek.

"Ok, I can't stay, your father wants to go eat at that little Mexican place in Tribeca," she said as she handed Nathan the bag.

"Thank you Ma, for everything you do for us." I smiled.

"Eht eht. What have I told you about that? This isn't a chore, it's a blessing." She smooshed Emma's cheeks together when she came and stood next to me.

"You go above and beyond."

"Oh please." She waved her hand. "Right now I just have to 'go'."

She laughed and stepped out into the elevator hall area. I closed the door once she got in the next available one.

"Did you eat?" I asked Emma.

"Yup. Aunt Kelly made baked ziti," she answered walking into the kitchen. She came out holding a bottle of water.

"Ok, drink up, then shower and teeth for you, missy," I told her.

"And Nate for me," Nathan said taking Nate from me.

I began to protest, only because he just got home after not seeing him all weekend but neither did Nathan, so.

"Here you go." I smiled. "Oh…and he needs a changing." I chuckled.

I made Nathan and me dinner while he fed Nate. Since the kid had started with the rice cereal in his bottles, he was beefing up and I loved it. Within the next two weeks, I planned to start making him solid baby food. Well, blender made solid food. Have you ever tasted the crap they call baby food? Ugh, absolutely no flavor. I think that's why Emma grew up to be a picky eater. That stuff was horrible.

After Nathan cleaned up the baby, he gave him a bath and put his son down just as dinner was ready. When Nathan came out to the kitchen, he was all smiles.

"Dinner's ready," I announced putting the plates on the counter. "What's with that smile?"

I laughed as he approached me.

"Just happy." He shrugged as he put a piece of chicken on his plate.

"It's chicken…nothing to get all emotional over," I teased him.

He kissed my head as he grabbed his fork.

By the time we were finished eating, both kids were out cold. Nate had been sleeping through the night for about two weeks so I knew I'd be in for an early morning. I decided to call it a night so I headed to the bedroom to get changed.

I heard Nathan enter the room as I began brushing my teeth.

"I feel like we just got out of bed," I joked.

"I make a lasting impression." He walked into the bathroom and picked up his toothbrush.

"Indeed," I said after I spit.

" Sexy." He laughed while he toothpasted up his toothbrush.

"I, too, make a lasting impression." I gave him a big cheesy smile, turned, and wiggled my butt as I walked out.

I went to go check on Nate one last time and kiss him goodnight since I didn't get to, before Nathan put him down. When I got back to the bedroom, Nathan was in bed texting or something on his phone. I climbed in over him and on to my side of the bed. He put his phone down and turned on his side to face me.

"Tired?" He asked with his arms folded across his chest and smiled up at me. I had picked up my lotion and started to put it on my legs when he began running his fingers up and down my arm.

"Stop, that tickles." I laughed as I pulled away.

"I know it does, that's the point."

"What, you trying to make another lasting impression?" We both laughed and his phone went off.

"Frank?" I asked as I rubbed the lotion in on my leg.

"No, it's Bristol," he said, so nonchalantly that I stopped what I was doing and turned my head to stare at him.

After a moment of him texting back and not realizing I was deadpanning darts at him, I cleared my throat to gain his attention.

"Who and why?" I asked.

"Bristol." He put his phone down and turned back on his side to face me.

"Why?" He asked.

I couldn't believe he was clueless as to why I was asking.

"I asked you first." I returned to my moisturizing.

"I texted her to let her know I hired Evelyn and I hoped it wasn't a problem for her."

"Ok...again...why?" I snapped this time.

"As a professional courtesy. What's your problem?" He crinkled his brow.

"Does she have a problem with it?" I ignored his question for the time being.

"No..." he answered.

"And if she did?" I asked in that 'choose your words carefully' tone.

"Then that's too bad?" He answered me as if he was asking if that was the right answer, which made me break out in laughter.

"Ahhh, that's good to know." I grabbed a tissue from my nightstand to wipe off the excess lotion from my hands and there it was...staring me in the face again.

The Journal.

I picked it up and sat Indian style with it in my hands.

"What? No pillow brigade tonight?" He laughed as he sat up.

"Shut it," I said as I took a pillow from behind me

and put it on my lap.

"Oh, well excuse me, I stand corrected." He chuckled and kissed the exposed skin on my shoulder as I opened the book.

July 29th

I've been getting out more and more, and remembering tidbits and chunks of myself with each passing day. I've been very careful with the company I keep. Charlie decided to tell the tabloids I was a man whore trying to take advantage of my 'situation'. My guess is she wasn't very happy I didn't call her again. Last week, a former costar, Lena, called. We met up for coffee. That was a confusing and awkward situation to say the least. She practically sat on my lap, touched me a lot, and held my hand when we were walking. At first, I thought it was a friendly thing but I don't think she did. That scenario was a nightmare for me to get a handle on. Especially with the photogs everywhere. Even if they're keeping their distance. Don't get me wrong the attention was nice and she is...holy Christ, she's smokin' hot...but something is off. Usually when a woman like that kisses you, you have some sort of response. Mentally, physically...something. I had nothing. It was like kissing a doorknob. That kiss made the front page of USWeekly, which sent Mom into a complete shit fit. Not in front of me, of course...but I heard her talking to someone on the phone about allowing her to talk to me about something. And how much of a stubborn and selfish woman she was being, but by the end of the call she'd told the person she loved 'em...which meant whoever it was on the other end of that call was important. When I asked her about it, she told me she was talking to Rachel about Tyler.

Lies. Something is up and I can FEEL it, not just see it. Feel it.

I was silent after I closed up the journal and stared at the ceiling while I gave myself a pep talk.

Well fuck. That sucked. That sucked big fat Kardashian ass is what that did. UGH. Stop shaking...get your shit together, Jordie.

I exhaled really loud and long then turned to him with a weak smile.

"Jordan, if this is too much...I didn't think..." he said, but I stopped him.

"I'm fine. Surprisingly enough I'm a lot better than I anticipated. Okay, yeah, that sucked. I didn't expect the whole handholding and the 'smokin' hot' part but it is what it is. I just keep reminding myself that you didn't know I existed."

I was looking down, fixated on my hands. I was fiddling with my rings.

"I didn't...and I can't begin to imagine how you felt having to see all of that without knowing the facts." He scooted up, and sat in front of me mirroring the way I was sitting.

"It's safe to assume it was you my mom was talking to that night?" He asked as he lifted my chin up to look at him.

"Yes," I whispered.

"How come you didn't want her to tell me about you, about us, Emma, the baby?" He asked.

And there we had it...the big Voldemort of questions...the one we had not spoken of...we'd just set sail into unchartered waters because this was taboo as far as I was concerned. It was the past...but again, I was trying to save Nathan from the pain of knowing what brought me to the decision to keep it all a secret.

"It's your turn Jordan. It's your turn to let it all out.

I'm okay, we're okay, our family is okay. You don't have to protect me anymore," he assured me.

"I hate when you do that shit." I gave him a small smile.

"Do what?" He cocked his head to the side in question.

"When you read my mind like that."

"So?" He took my hands in his.

"There were a few reasons. At first, it was because I didn't want to cause you more confusion. You didn't know who you were, and I was going to throw at you, an almost wife, a step kid, and a baby on the way? It's not my style. I wasn't doing that to you. Then as you began to remember more and more but not me, or us, and I saw you continually going on dates and being affectionate with other women, I decided it was what was best for everyone. Move on with my life and you regain your life."

I sniffled because I was starting to tear up like a big fat sissy.

"You were going to keep my child a secret from me because I was dating?"

I could tell, by his expression, he didn't know how to react to that. He looked torn between pissed and confused.

"Don't look at me like that Nathan. You don't understand…" I started to say, but he cut me off.

"You're damn right I don't understand." His eyebrows mashed together.

All right, he was pissed not confused.

We were both silent for a moment or two.

"Help me understand. I know it wasn't out spite or anything like that. At least I *hope* it wasn't." He rubbed the top of my hand with his thumb.

I could tell he was doing his best to keep it together and stay calm.

"When you were in the hospital...after it first happened. You said some pretty shitty things to me. They hurt and they stuck with me. So, after that, I went through *great* lengths to keep it a secret. I mean, Frank and Todd had to pay off the paps, and the police report was buried with Hoffa I assume, because nobody ever got a hold of it. Jason wasn't having a public trial since the military was dealing with him so...it was just easier to leave well enough alone. You wouldn't have to relive the incident and pretend you knew who I was, let alone love me and have a baby on the way." I saw his face ease up a bit.

"What did I say?" He asked.

Fuck, fuck, triple fuck. I didn't want to do this.

"Well, you pretty much said that you didn't know me...that you couldn't have kids because you were sterile so the baby wasn't yours, and if I wasn't going to 'blow you' I should leave. That's all I remember, because I blacked out after that. Oh, and I was hot, and from the looks of my face I liked it rough." I began to sob after I said the last part.

I thought about how I reacted last night and how all I wanted to do was jump on Nathan to show him how much I loved him. How I couldn't have him close enough to me. Tonight, I just wanted to cry.

The thought of Lena's lips on his made my skin crawl and my stomach curl inward. I hadn't cried sad tears in a long time. It had been all happy fucking trails since he came back to me...and now...just like he'd said...it was my turn. He put it out there for me to understand where his head was at during that time. It was my turn to let him know where my heart was at during that same time.

He moved to sit next to me. He pulled me onto his lap and just let me cry. He didn't say anything; he simply rubbed my arm, moved the hair out of my face, or kissed me lightly somewhere until I cried myself to sleep. Two nights, two different reactions...we were in for one hell of a rollercoaster ride.

Nate woke up around a quarter after five and Emma shortly after. Nathan slept in a bit. I didn't wake him until I got Emma off to school. It was Evelyn's first day so I figured he should be awake for it.

As expected, she was knocking on the door at eight-thirty on the dot. When I opened the door to let her in, I was surprised. Not only had she sounded like a different person, she looked like one as well. Natural make up, hair up, and she traded her girl's night out dress for a pair of denim skinny jeans, black wedge heeled mid-calf knee boots, and a gray ribbed turtleneck under a black faux fur vest.

I couldn't help but like her. She was the complete opposite of the woman I encountered Friday night at the bar. Once Nathan came out from the bedroom, I let him take over.

"No, I don't like to go to the Starbucks across the street. You see the young man who has a massive crush on my wife is trying to kill me." Nathan said obnoxiously loud as he passed by the kitchen with Evelyn.

"That is not true or funny, Nathan," I yelled out to them. I heard him laugh.

"And this is the conference/media room..." His voice trailed off down the hallway.

Oh, how I love that man.

CHAPTER 13

Friday came quick. Surprisingly enough, I accomplished a lot. I'll be the first to admit that since we moved, life had been so much less chaotic but I didn't want to say it out loud but it was…normal. I mean right down to being able to walk outside our building and not have a mob scene of paparazzi and fans. The fans weren't a problem most of the time anway, but the photographers were relentless.

Evelyn's first week of work went flawlessly. She knew people Nathan didn't even know and by Wednesday, it was as if she had been his assistant for years.

"Good morning Evelyn," I said to her when I answered the door.

"Morning." She smiled as she walked in.

I shuffled over to the table still wearing my kitty cat slippers, yoga capris and a t-shirt.

"Girl, you lookin' rough this morning." Evelyn snorted, pouring herself some coffee.

"What the fuck?" Shocked, I laughed and turned

around in my chair. "That accent is really happening today eh?" I followed her with my eyes as she sat down at the table with me and took a sip of her coffee.

"It's Friday, I'm letting loose a bit." She gave a small fake laugh.

"Oh is that what it is? Liar," I accused her jokingly.

"I just had a very heated conversation with someone and when my temper flares it takes me a bit of time to cool off. If you'd like to send me home…"

"What? Why? No…of course not. Go home for being yourself? Please. I don't know who you worked for in the past…well, I do but you know what I mean…Nathan isn't like that."

"Nathan isn't, but let's call a spade a spade here…it's *your* opinion that calls the shots around here so…" She grinned and took another sip of her coffee.

"I knew I liked you for a reason." I laughed. "And no, I'm not like that either."

I smiled.

Her work cell rang and she took the call, so I opened up my laptop to check out the daily gossip. Same ol' shit, it was just a different story line. The newest fabrication, in the 'Fabulous life of Nordie' as I liked to call it, stated that I was keeping Nathan on a short leash so his encounters with Bristol were far and few between.

"Ha," I shouted, then threw my hand over my mouth wide-eyed because I forgot Evelyn was on the phone. She gave me a 'what' face, so I turned the screen towards her so she could see the headline.

"Idiots…," she said and rolled her eyes.

"No, I'm sorry, not you, Mr. McDaniels." She stifled a laugh.

"Alright, see you at one pm on Thursday. Give the doorman your name, he'll let you up." She paused, and nodded her head in approval." Yes, sir. Thank you,

you too. Goodbye." She ended the call.

"McDaniels over at ABC?" I asked not taking my eyes off my screen.

"No, his son over at OneFilm," she answered as she typed something in on her iPad.

"Oh?" That got my attention.

I always got a sinking feeling in my stomach whenever I knew Nathan might have a job lined up. I knew it was his job and all, but we didn't need any more money, and well...I hated when he left us or got to kiss other women. I *hated* that he kissed other women and had to grind all over them sometimes. I don't watch his movies either. I guess that's why Hollywood married Hollywood because everyone had kissed each other at one point or another. Me, I wasn't buying the idea.

"Chill Jordie, I see your pulse throbbing out of that skinny ass neck of yours," she snorted. "It's just a meeting about the release of 'Rover Field'."

"*My* skinny ass neck?" I laughed. "That's about the only skinny thing on me these days." I wrapped my hands around my throat.

"Whateva.'" She stood and put her cup in the sink.

"Good morning ladies." Nathan walked into the kitchen holding Nate and kissed me on the head before handing him to me. He went to pour himself a cup of coffee.

"Evelyn, I didn't expect to see you in here," he said as he put sugar in his coffee.

I looked at her confused, and she shrugged her shoulders just as bewildered.

"Um...why not? Do I have Fridays off or something?" She questioned.

"No." Nathan turned and leaned against the counter. "I just expected to see Rosie Perez in here is all. I thought I heard her talking." He snickered playfully as he raised his mug to his mouth.

I busted out laughing with Evelyn joining me.

"Nice boss. Real nice." She threw a crumpled napkin at him.

"Just keepin' it real," he teased and pushed off the counter.

She laughed and rolled her eyes.

"Anyhow, you have a nine-fifteen video conference with Eidenberg. He needs to go over some reshoot possibilities. Then at one-thirty, you have to meet with JP down at Naomi's salon. You're getting a haircut and wardrobe run through for upcoming events."

"I don't want to try on clothes," Nathan whined and stomped his foot.

"A temper tantrum. Really Nathan?" I chuckled.

"You aren't trying anything on. Just getting a glimpse of what's to come," Evelyn reassured him.

"Oh, okay." He smiled like he'd won an argument, little did he know he'd be trying on every single suit. He then kissed Nate on the head and bent down to kiss me. Between the series of small kisses he was giving me, he said 'I. Love. You.' Then he headed out of the kitchen, Evelyn on his heels.

"Love you, too."

I lifted Nate up so he was eye level with me and started that stupid baby talk thing I do with him. "And I love you, too," I cooed and raspberried his cheek. The sound of his laughter was the greatest sound ever.

After a bath for Nate, and a shower for me, we emerged fresh and ready for the day at nine-twenty. Fiona would be here shortly to pick up Nate and I was so thankful because I had errands to run. I always felt bad toting him around while I ran here and there. I would rather he be with his grandparents getting some brain stimulation and activity rather in a car seat carrier all damn day.

When they arrived to pick him up, I told Fiona she wouldn't have to worry about getting Emma to Kelly's because I wanted to have a family weekend. As I kissed them goodbye, Rachel came barging through the front door in tears.

"Oh Christ," I mumbled.

I wasn't prepared to deal with this. Nathan had *just* told me about Tyler's plan to pop the question so I hadn't come up with a reassuring excuse yet.

"Rachel, sweetheart, what's wrong?" Fiona asked concerned.

"It's Tyler. He's cheating on me," she stammered through her words and wailed out.

We were all sort of dumbfounded because it was a solar flare in the east wind on the third Tuesday of every century when you saw Rachel cry, let alone go full blown emotional basket case.

"Oh, Rachel. That is just ridiculous." Fiona waved her hand. "That boy is nuts about you. You're everything to him. I was just talking to his mother the other night. She called to ask about a rest…"

"She called to find out about a good remedy to get some rest right? Me too. She called here asking how I was getting a full night's rest with the baby being up. I told her I was lucky to have a brilliant caring mother-in-law who helps me out." I gave her the wide-eyed 'stop talking' look.

"Yes, lucky you," Fiona said.

Thank god, she got the message.

"Anyhow, Rachel, I'm sure you're just being overly sensitive. Are you due for your period?" Fiona asked, and I busted out laughing at Rachel's facial expression.

"What? No. What kind of question is that Fiona?"

Rachel said before she blew her nose.

"A legitimate one. Women tend to get a bit more emotional before their cycles." She shrugged at me like she had no idea what to do.

"Ok, time to stop talking," I snorted and gave Fiona the go ahead to leave with a kiss to Nate and a gentle arm behind the back to guide her along.

"Bye kids." Fiona gave Rachel a sheepish smile and left.

"What the fuck? My period? I love her and all Jords, but for reals...she doesn't know what she's talking about."

"Okay, so what's up?" I dragged her over to the couch and made her sit with me.

"Okay, so I was opening the mail and I opened Tyler's AMEX Bill instead of mine. When I realized it was his and went to put it down, I noticed some hotel charges for the Ritz fucking Carlton, Jordan...the fucking Ritz," she yelled and threw her bag on the ground.

I went to pick it up because it was a beautiful MK bag but she slapped my hand and said don't. I looked up at her startled; her face was bright red, full of snot and tears. She reminded me of me that night Nathan left my apartment the first time. Only she could walk and well, function.

"Rachel, I'm sure it's for a gig or something. Maybe a label is coming in from LA to see him play and he got a room trying to impress them?" I blurted out.

Damn girl, not too shabby for spur of the moment.

"The charges are for a reservation. When I called today, the woman told me it was booked for next weekend. The penthouse suite." She sobbed.

"He told me he had a gig Friday night late so he wouldn't be at the bar to take me home." She cried harder and dragged out her sentence in a loud whine.

"Did you ask Nathan about it?" She shot at me and leaned in close.

"What? No. You told me not to," I said.

"Why the fuck not? You never listen to me, why did you decide to start now?"

"Okay Rach, calm down. You're a little hysterical…," I started, but she went off on a tangent of this is why she hates love…men suck, they always leave.

Her dad had left her and her mom, and her only other real relationship ran off with some SoHo tramp back in 2004 so it had left her a bit jaded…and now there was Tyler with his secrets. I've never experienced being dumped…unless having a fiancé not having any recollection of you, or your unborn child, counts. I can imagine the experience would leave someone very jaded.

When I first started dating Jason, he had just broken it off with his long time sweetheart after six years, Brianna Stolten. She was a year younger than him. Anyhow, she would call him every once in a while. I'd see the Santa Anna TX number pop up on the caller ID, and I'd laugh. Honestly, I didn't really give a shit but I heard her cry and beg him to come back to her while he laughed and told her how pathetic she was. I should have seen the signs then that he was a fucking maniac. Now I had to try to make my best friend not feel that same pain. There was no way to convince her otherwise, without telling her the truth. Just as I was about to start spilling the beans, Nathan walked in the room.

"What the hell is that noise? Rachel? Was that you? What the fuck is wrong with you and what is that noise you're making?" He looked so confused.

"She opened Tyler's credit card statement by accident and saw charges for the penthouse at the Ritz

Carlton for next weekend." I gave him the 'eek' face.

"Oh, that? I arranged for a music director to fly in and discuss the possibility of getting some of his tracks onto a soundtrack or two. I told him to pay for the room and I'd reimburse him." Nathan was calm and collected, not a single hitch in his voice.

Damn he's good, and on the same page as me.

"Then why didn't he tell me?" She asked beginning to calm down.

"If I know Tyler, and I do, since I was fifteen, he didn't want to get his hopes up, or jinx it or have you show up and make him nervous. He'd rather hide it than ask you not to come to show him support and risk hurting your feelings. You know?" He shrugged as Rachel sat up straight and stopped crying completely.

"Yeah, I guess." She sniffled.

Holy shit. He pulled it off.

"Stop that crying and go wash your face." Nathan gave her a head nod towards the bathroom. "While she does that I have to go back and assure Eidenberg that a cat was, indeed, not on fire out here."

He turned to head back down the hallway.

"Hey," I said to get his attention back over to me.

"Thank you," I mouthed when he turned around.

"You're welcome," he mouthed back, and winked.

Frank was picking me up around noon to run some errands. I headed to Evelyn's office so I could let her know I was going across the street for coffee and meeting Frank downstairs. I was digging through my purse for my keys when I walked through the door.

"Hey Ev, can you let Nathan know that…" I stopped when I noticed she closed her laptop really fast when I entered.

"Nobody cares if you're online while you're working. It's not like you're a slacker or anything." I went back to digging in my bag.

"Oh...oh okay, thank you." She gave what sounded like to me a nervous laugh as she put her laptop to the side and placed some files on top of it.

"Anyhow, you were saying?" She asked when she was finished tidying up the spot.

"Oh, yeah. I'm leaving. Tell Nathan for me, please. I'll be back here for Emma so he doesn't have to rush with Naomi and JP."

I looked up and pulled my keys out. "Damn, finally."

"No problem, I'll see you Monday, have a great weekend," she said to me as she stood up.

"Oh and here," I said to her, as I twisted a key off my key ring.

"What's this for?" She asked looking confused.

"Elevator key." I smiled. "You can't stop on the floor without the front desk letting you up, or one of these."

I handed it to her.

"Jordie, I don't mind signing in everyday..."

"No, don't be silly. I know it can be a pain in the ass waiting for them." I cut her off and placed the key on her desk.

"Have a nice weekend." I hurried out the door before she could refuse again.

Frank and I pulled up to the building just as Emma's car was dropping her off. I knew Nathan would be back soon and the in-laws would be back any minute with Nate. I hustled up to the apartment to get the groceries put away and talk to Emma before the baby got home. Poor kid has been taking the whole change like a champ. She'd turned ten, and it was a kick in the ass to me...my baby girl was not so much baby as she was girl now. Ten...and here I was doing it all over again. She was still spending weekends at my sister's house in Jersey but I really wanted her to start staying home at least two weekends a month from now on. She used to have to go to Kelly's because I worked all weekend but I don't anymore so, there's no reason for it.

My sister said I was being selfish and disrupting the order in her life. She had friends there and kids she enjoyed. Maybe I was being selfish, or maybe I just felt like a terrible mom because I shipped my daughter off to New Jersey every weekend for no reason. Either way, I was a terrible mom. If I let her continue to go, *I* felt guilty and if I didn't let her go, I was the meanest mom in the world and she'd be at home but miserable.

Damned if you do, damned if you don't.

As I put the bags on the kitchen table, Emma started to dig through one and when I turned from putting the milk in the fridge, she was in a new bag.

"What are you looking for?" I asked as I put the cereal up.

She looked at me as if I had two heads.

"I asked you to pick me up my own razor. Remember?" She said with a duhhh face.

"You're ten. No," I answered her.

"Just because I'm ten doesn't mean I'm not a hairy wilda-beast, Mom. Look at my legs...for real, it's embarrassing." She stuck her leg out and pulled down her knee high sock to mid-calf.

"Holy shit, Emma." I covered my mouth because I hadn't meant to say it out loud, but it just came out.

"Thanks Mom, I told you." She sulked and pulled her sock back up.

"It's just because it's so dark, sweetie. If it wasn't, it wouldn't be so bad." I went back to putting up the groceries.

"Yeah, well it *is* that dark. One kid called me Chewbacca, and another asked if I was French." She pulled out a chair, plopped in it and slouched down.

"You aren't shaving your legs yet Emma, so drop it." I closed the cabinet and gathered all the bags together to put in the pantry.

"I'm going to pack." She stood in a huff and slid the chair back in excessively loud.

"For what?" I turned to her.

"Aunt Kelly's." She had a little bit too much sass in her voice for my taste.

"You're staying home this weekend. It's family weekend." I leaned against the counter.

"What? You're kidding me, right? What am I going to do here all weekend, Mom? I have no friends on this side of town and everyone always wants to come here because of Naaathan." She mocked and rolled her eyes.

"Emma Lynn," I scolded her.

"Jordan Marie," she spit back at me.

I stared at her blankly. At that point, Frank whistled, gave me a look, and walked out of the room. I don't know if I was more pissed off because of her attitude or the fact that she was right.

"Listen to me very carefully," I annunciated each word staccato.

She stared blankly at me.

"Your attitude sucks Emma. You have some very valid points but you're getting them across the wrong way. I have no clue as to why that sassy ass mouth of yours decided it was a good idea to speak to your mother in that manner but it's unacceptable. I will *allow* you to go to Aunt Kelly's because you do have a point," I said, and she started to walk away but I stopped her by tugging on the top of her sleeve. "I'm not finished. This is a onetime pass. I am giving you the chance to know that this was unacceptable behavior and you will not speak to me like that again. Because if you do, Frank as my witness..."

"Leave me out of this," Frank called from the living room and I had to stifle a laugh.

"I promise you, Emma, the outcome will not be in your favor."

"Yes, Mom." She sulked.

I knew she felt bad.

"I love you." I let go of her sleeve and she hugged me.

"Love you, too." She moped as she walked out of the kitchen.

CHAPTER 14

So much for my family weekend, it was Friday night and it was just Nathan and me. Emma went to Kelly's and Nate stayed with the in-laws. I wasn't complaining. It's what made everyone happy. If they were happy, I was happy.

Nathan had gotten home about six from Naomi's salon and I sure as hell didn't feel like cooking so I ordered us some sushi.

After we ate, I cleaned the kitchen while Nathan finished up a few things in his media room. I tossed the last of the paper towel roll in the trash and headed down to get in some comfy clothes. The girls needed to breathe. I changed, grabbed my laptop, and plopped down on the chaise.

"Alright internets, let's see what sort of cracked out shit you're talking tonight," I said to myself as I clicked on 'Nate-Nation' from my favorites.

" Oh, look at that, little Miss Kookoo Pants is at it again." I scoffed. "I wonder what's in her bucket of crazy today."

I scrolled though the normal haters, lovers, and 'I-dont-carers', who actually do care but strangely enough say they don't. I mean they must care because they're always in the middle of it somehow. I also noticed on my choo-choo train ride through crazy town that the lovers were on the same playing field as the haters. They would go back and forth, arguing over something that either never happened, was never going to happen or they wanted to happen. It was as if they actually knew what went on in our lives. As if they knew Nathan sits in front of the TV while I cook him some gourmet meal, while I hold Nate on my hip with one hand and then serve it to him on the couch after tucking a napkin in his shirt as a bib or some shit like that. As if we are the perfect little couple.

Sometimes it made me laugh. Sometimes it just made me scared. What made them think they knew us at all? Queen Crazy Pants herself Deloony posted all the pics that the paps took of Nathan with everyone at Naomi's salon.

Oh my, but he does look nice in that suit.

I continued to scroll through the pics and stopped at a video that a fan took of Nathan posing and meeting a few fans before going inside the salon. He looked so happy interacting with them. I noticed Evelyn was behind Nathan on the phone pacing back and forth. She said something really loud but I couldn't make out what it was over the noise in the video.

I rewound it a few seconds and turned it up a little. When that didn't work, I tried to read her lips. I could make out, "Knock it the fuck off." I wondered what it was about for like a second, then closed up the laptop and put it to the side.

Why was I watching videos of my man when I could be making videos with my man?

I hopped up and practically skipped down the hall to

where my husband was in the 'media' room. That fucker had a huge table...and if I had my way, we were about to find out how many angles the cameras could capture.

"Hey," I said as I walked in the room.

I'd heard him talking earlier but I didn't realize he was actually on a Skype call with someone. Thank god, I was wearing pants.

"Okay Bill, let me get going. We can discuss the details next week. Call my assistant and let her know what records and receipts I'll need," he rushed out the words to our CPA, Bill.

"Hello, Jordan," Bill's voice greeted me through the speakers.

"Hey Billy." I went and stood behind Nathan. "How's Mel and the kids?"

"Everyone's well, thank you. It's nice to see you. We'll all have to do an adult dinner sometime," he answered. "Sure will," I agreed.

"Alright man, catch ya' later," Nathan said hitting a button before turning in his chair to face me.

"Remind me to thank the inventor of yoga pants," Nathan said as he slid his hands past my hips and groped my behind.

"Funny you should mention my pants." I wiggled my butt and rested my arms on his shoulders.

"Oh? Why's that?" He grinned as he slipped his hand under the hem of my shirt and lifted it a little exposing my belly button. He began to kiss my stomach and worked his way up as his rose from the chair.

Huh? Why's what? Oh.

"Because I came in here to get you in them," I said leaning my head to the side to let him access my neck.

Sweet Jesus.

August 12th

Making new/old friends is great. Tyler and Rachel took me out to eat one night, and the waitress was cute so I saw no harm in asking her out for drinks or whatever came to mind afterwards. Before she could even answer, Rachel made a remark about me waiting until my rash clears up before I get back out there. What the fuck it was about was out of my realm of comprehension...but it sure pissed me off.

Mom and Dad have to go back to Sacramento for a week or so, real soon. She wants me to come with them. I don't want to hurt her feelings but I need a break from her. Dad's motto is 'It is what it is and what will be, will be'. Mom doesn't seem to get that. Things are also getting tense between us so it'll be good for her to be away from me for a while. For now, I've stopped asking what happened. If I haven't remembered by now there's a reason I don't remember because the puzzle is slowly getting put together day by day. More and more comes back to me...sometimes it's a smell, sometimes it's nothing in particular but it just pops in there. I've come to terms with the fact that there was a reason my brain doesn't want to me to know. Whenever I ask anyone I go out with, they just tell me that nobody really knows what happened. Just that I was shot and lost my memory. Besides, the women I hang out with, most of them are really, great ladies, but by the third outing, I realize that something isn't there and the void inside remains empty.

August 14th

Today Tyler took me over to the studio. I've been in talks to start working again soon. I've been looking at projects and what not, but I'm still not cleared to drive. They suspended my license for six months. The doctors said it's a mandatory precaution because I had a seizure in the hospital. I think it's a mandatory pain in my ass. Mom and Dad are leaving for Sacramento tomorrow. I have a date tomorrow night. I met her at the gym over at the studio. She works in the legal department. She seems nice enough, so I asked.

Tyler says I need to slow down. I guess to him, it looks like I actually am being a man-whore, fucking every hot chick I see. I'm just hoping to get some quality alone time with a woman. It's been so difficult knowing there are people watching you at all times. If it isn't the paps, it's Frank, if it isn't Frank, it's Mom, if it isn't Mom, it's Tyler. And it's CONSTANTLY.

Let's see how this one goes.

August 15th

It's 9:10 PM and I'm home from my date. Yes, already!

I wanted to get out of the city to a place a little less expected, so Frank said he had the perfect spot. It was a pizza joint over in the East Village. That part of town was like its own little world. So many people but not too crowded. When I got out of the car to help Sadie (the chick I met in the gym), something caught my eye. Well, not exactly caught my eye, actually it was more like a flash of something. By the time I realized it, I was staring at the 'PIZZA' sign, Frank was in front of me with Sadie on my right. I was frozen...completely blank. Then suddenly, it was like somebody shook my head and scrambled everything around again. I couldn't focus and I felt like running because the void in my gut was swallowing me whole. I kissed Sadie on the cheek, apologized to her, and asked Frank to take her home.

Something about that place was a game changer for

me. I walked around for what felt like hours but didn't know what it was. I stopped in a bike shop and bought one to ride around on. Something important is there. I just have to figure out what.

August 16th

   Frank came to pick me up this morning. I stopped at Tyler's. His girlfriend went postal that I showed up unannounced. Something about what if she'd had company or hadn't cleaned. I reassured her that I didn't mind and as far as company, I told her I don't bite people but she just stood there. It was pretty evident Rachel was not happy about it, but I'm glad she wasn't because if she hadn't been, she wouldn't have thrown a boot at Tyler and then I wouldn't have remembered a boot just like it...blood stains and all.

   When I picked it up, Rachel just stared at me...HARD. Like she was trying to send me some kind of telepathic message...or shrink my head. It was very strange. Tyler took the boot and laughed. When I asked about a boot with a blood stain, Rachel's whole demeanor changed. She smiled at me and began to talk, but Tyler quickly interrupted. Rachel rolled her eyes and left the room.

   Rachel knows more than what everyone's letting on. I know she'll crack. She's one to spontaneously combust if you shake her up enough.

   Later, I went for a bike ride and ended up back at the pizzeria. I was hungry so I went in for a slice. The waiter asked how I was doing like he knew me. He asked where my bodyguard was. Why he would give a shit about that is beyond me? But he did tell me that Frank could be a scary guy.

   I rode my bike around. Up and down the streets. Three hours later, I was sitting on a street bench on East 13th street. I didn't know why.

I put Nathan's journal back in its normal place on my nightstand after I closed it. I wanted to slam it shut but I refrained.

"Is it getting any easier for you?" Nathan took my hand and raised it to his lips.

"I feel like I should be saying yes..." I responded in a hushed voice.

"I feel like you should be saying exactly how you feel." He kissed my hand and put it on his stomach.

"Okay then. Yes, and no. Yes, because I am getting used to the fact that there were other women...and no, because I get the same desperate pit in my stomach every time I read something about one of them. Make sense?" I peered over at him.

"Perfect sense." He exhaled and stared up at the ceiling. "Would you like to continue?"

"Stop asking me the same shit every time I'm done. I'll let you know when I've had enough," I snapped, then swung myself so I was sitting on the edge of the bed and looked for my pants.

"I'll take that as a no," he mumbled.

"Why?" I stood and headed to the bathroom.

"Because you're walking away." He gestured with his hand.

"I have to pee, Nathan. Jesus Christ." I spun around to look at him.

He had raked both his hands through his hair and was grabbing two fistfuls while a long seemingly frustrated rumble erupted from the back of his throat.

"My god, you frustrate the hell out of me, Jordan." He jerked his hands from his hair, slapped them on his lap, and exhaled loudly.

"I can see how my need to urinate can be distressingly frustrating to you."

I rolled my eyes and slammed the bathroom door behind me. I hurried up and peed because I knew he'd be walking through the bathroom door at any moment. Just as I flushed, he came in just as I expected.

"Sorry," Nathan said as he leaned on the wall next to the open door.

"You have nothing to apologize for Nathan."

I reached into the shower to hit the button that turned it on. It was one of those fancy mammojamos, where you wave your hand by the sensor then adjust the temperature digitally. Or in my case hit the button number one, the one already programmed to my preferred water temperature. Talk about ostentatious.

Nathan stuck his hand in and hit the number three button, which meant a shower for two coming up. That was our agreed upon temperature. I wrapped my hair up in a signature Jordie half-assed bun and waited for the beep. Just like an oven, it fucking beeped when it pre-heated to the proper temperature. I eyed Nathan carefully as he undressed. I had to choose my words wisely because I didn't want him to take the journal away from me, but at the same time I didn't like the direction it was heading in.

I stepped in a few seconds shy of the beep and Nathan followed.

"You know what I was just thinking?" I said to him as I grabbed the soap.

"What's that?" He answered while he wet his hair.

"I'm afraid if you don't like what I have to say about something in your journal you're going to take it away from me." I lathered up my arms.

"That's ridiculous. You don't think I took that into consideration beforehand, Jordie? Of course I weighed the ramifications of sharing it with you, but I told you already I know you can handle it." He began to shampoo his hair so he wasn't looking at me.

"That's great but not what I'm saying. I know I can handle it...but can you deal with me the way I handle things?"

He opened his eyes, stared at the ceiling, and stopped washing his hair for a moment.

"If you and I could get through that, we can get through anything. So, yeah, I'll be okay." He started to rinse.

"Just as long as we're on the same page...no pun intended." I hip checked him, and he grabbed me around my waist and pulled me close.

"I hope we're on the same page." He leaned in and kissed me.

"Hold on Tiger..." I looked down because I could feel him against me. "Woods." We both laughed.

" No pun intended?" He smirked.

"Oh no, pun intended." I tippy toed up to kiss him.

"You know, Rachel told me about the day you stopped by there unannounced. She really thought you would remember at like any moment, once you saw my boots. She wanted it to happen so badly. Everyone was tired of seeing me a total mess." I turned away from him so he could wash my back.

"Well, it's not like you made it easy for me to remember Jordan." He snickered playfully. "You wouldn't let anyone talk about you. Frank had to pay off every media outlet to *not* mention you at all, and then threw a medical gag order at the ones who didn't want to comply. The mental damage I could endure by being force fed the barest of information about us and you being pregnant, it was as if everyone thought it could set off some emotional chain reaction and Nathan goes boom." He rattled off in one quick sentence as his hands rounded to the front of me sliding over my breasts.

I leaned my head back on his chest and closed my eyes.

"I had my reasons Nathan, mainly because I didn't

want you to 'go boom'," I said to him.

"What if I'd never remembered? Were you going to just never tell me about Nate?" He slid his hands down to my waist and kept them there.

I opened my eyes and stared off in silence. *Uht-oh...*

"Tick tock, tick tock." He nudged into me from behind.

"I didn't think that far ahead. It was a cross that bridge when we got there type of thing, ya' know?" I said in a shaky voice.

"You okay?" He turned me around.

"Yeah." I paused. "I'm hungry."

I lied.

"I love you, Jordan. No matter what." His eyes locked with mine.

Lord, what those blue eyes still did to my insides.

"I love you too," I replied.

CHAPTER 15

I was sex spent and pleasantly sore by the time Sunday morning rolled around. Nathan and I had one hell of a weekend together. I love my children more than anything but I was willing to sacrifice the weekends with them if it made everyone happy. Sure, I missed them but it was only a day and a half really and it was worth it. Everyone got a mental break.

Emma was going to be home around noon and Fiona was on her way back with the baby. Nathan made waffles so when I got out of the shower, it was all I could smell in the air. This girl loved her husband's waffles.

"Smells *so* good," I said to Nathan when I walked in the kitchen.

I hopped up on the counter next to where he was waffle making and my shirt hitched up to where he could see my panties.

"As much as I'd like to have you for breakfast, I regretfully have to resist and ask you to put some pants on." He bent and kissed the top of my thigh and looked back up with a smile.

Look at his eyes. Yum. What I...

"Jordan." He snapped his finger and chuckled.

"Yeah? What? Huh?" I sat up straight, wide eyed then laughed. "Okay why do I need pants? I have at least an hour before Mom gets here with Nate."

"Because we are having a guest in about thirty minutes, so pants and then eat up," he said as he put a waffle on the plate for me.

"Who? And waffle first, pants later." I hopped off the counter and grabbed my plate.

I took the butter and the syrup off the counter to the table with me and plopped in my chair.

"Do you want coffee?" he asked me.

"Ya. Thanks." I slapped some butter on my waffle then picked up the syrup.

"So?" I asked again as I squeezed out the sticky goodness all over my breakfast.

"Bristol," he said as he placed the coffee mug in front of me.

I stopped squeezing. My sticky goodness was at a drip now and I had no words for a moment.

"Babe?" He laughed and bent over to look at me.

"Uh, why?" I muttered.

"She wanted to talk to us, so I invited her over since we really can't go anywhere with the kids coming home soon."

"Uh-huh." I cut a piece of waffle with my fork then harpooned it.

"I was going to go meet up with her but she said she needed to talk to you, too. Since one of us has to be here, I improvised. Is that a problem?"

His tone changed to that 'I-am-man' tone and every nerve in my body came alive. All I wanted to do was jump him at that point. I loved it when he got all neanderthalish on me.

"No, sir." I stabbed another piece of my waffle.

When I finished, I went to get some pants on and came back to Nathan at the door.

"Be nice," he said as he glanced back at me before he opened it.

I rolled my eyes at him.

"I'm always nice." I smiled sweetly.

"Uh-huh." He grinned as he opened the door.

"Bristol…and uh Mike? Hey…there."

Nathan turned back and looked at me with a 'what the fuck' expression on his face. I stood frozen, jaw dropped.

"Hey…guys. What's up?" I managed to sputter out.

I hoped I didn't sound too shocked.

"Jordie, so nice to see you." Bristol stepped in and Mike followed her.

"Hey Jords," Mike said. He looked uncomfortable.

"I'm so sorry to bother you on a Sunday but this needed to be worked out ASAP," she said handing Mike her coat and taking a seat on the couch.

"What needs working out? And please, have a seat." Nathan said sarcastically as he closed the door and stood next to me.

We exchanged another high browed wide eye WTF look.

"Well, I've asked Mike to be my bodyguard, and I wan…" she began to say but I cut her off.

"But he already has a job. A job he's been at for nearly ten years." My voice rose and my teeth clenched tight as I finished the sentence.

"And that's great but where's the opportunity for him? Ten years is a long time to be a bouncer." She put her hand on his arm.

"No offense sweetie." Bristol added looking up at

Mike. He nodded, stone faced.

"Mike? Is this what you want? I mean obviously it must be if you're here…with her…on a Sunday." I lifted my hand up in question then slapped it down on my leg in a huff.

Yeah, I was pissed.

"Is this about Evelyn, Bristol? Because if it is, I didn't ask you to fi…" I began.

"No, this isn't about Evelyn. This is about an opportunity for Michael to have a career. To move up in the world," she said in a flat tone then gave me the closed eye roll to comeback and stare at me blankly.

This bitch, and Michael? She calls him Michael?

"Well, whatever the hours are I guess you'll have to work around the weekends. Mike, I *need* you on weekends." I heard my octaves and decibels crank up with every sentence.

"Calm down Jordan," Nathan said putting his hand on my back trying to soothe me.

"I'm afraid I'll need him weekends," Bristol picked her cuticle and never looked up at me.

"And I'm afraid that…"

"Jordie, I want to take the job." Mike interrupted me.

I stood there dumbfounded for a moment just staring at Mike in disbelief. Then I caught a glimpse of Bristol's bitch grin, looking at her freshly picked cuticles with her hand stretched out in front of her.

"I guess that settles it. You start this week." She stood, still never making eye contact with Nathan or me.

"What? This weekend? I can't possibly find a replacement by then and the law requires me to have at least two security guys, Bristol," I yelled.

"What? I can't this weekend, Bristol, she needs a replacement," Mike said at the same time I did.

"This weekend, Michael, take it or leave it." She took her jacket from him and her hand lingered on his before she slid it off.

"Take it," He said sullenly and looked over at me.

"I'm sorry Jordan. It's just time I move on with my life. You don't need me anymore." He put his hand on the small of Bristol's back and led her towards the door.

"Mike, of course I need you. I don't understand."

I was truly fucking lost at that moment.

"Jordie. It's okay. Let him go. Frank will know someone who can fill in on short notice," Nathan said to me but had locked eyes with Mike.

"Well, then don't fucking bother coming in all week if you're going to leave me high and dry," I screeched at Mike.

I folded my arms and whole-heartedly waited for him to change his mind. This was Mike after all. He'd been with me since day one. The first day I bought the bar, I put a help wanted sign on the door until I could run an ad and he showed up looking for a part time job. Which eventually lead to a full time one. He's been with me for nine and a half years for Christ's sake. There was no fucking way he would leave me. Especially not, like this.

"If that's what you want Jordan. I understand. Just let Rachel know I'll be by Friday for my pay." He put his hand on the knob to open the door and looked back at me.

"It was a good run boss. Give Emma a hug for me," Mike said softly.

"Oh Jesus Christ, just open the door. Let's go, I'm starving. Glad we had this chat. Nate I'm sure I'll see you soon. Thanks for your understanding, Jordie. It's so much easier when it's amicable." She gave us that bitch grin and walked out the door to the elevator.

"Mike," my voice reeked of desperation and sadness.

"Take care, Jordie. Nate." He looked at Nathan and nodded. Nathan nodded back.

"Take care, Mike," Nathan said walking over to the door.

I felt the tears start to form and my nose began to sting.

"Fucking bitch," I screamed out after he closed it, and I began to cry.

Later after the kids got home, we sat and talked a bit with Emma going over her weekend. It wasn't until after we'd eaten, showered, and readied for bed that I finally stopped seething. I tried to hide it but I spent the night banging shit around, and huffing and puffing. Yeah, I don't do so well with subtle, not to mention muttering shit to myself. I must have sounded like I had Tourette's or something. I was cursing up a shit storm.

I came out of the bathroom and plopped on the chaise to moisturize my legs, still muttering, of course. Nathan was in bed already watching something on NatGeo.

"Bitch," I blurted out.

Well, I thought I was done being mad. I saw Nathan pick up the remote and shut the TV off.

"Ready to talk about it?" he asked and motioned for me to come to bed.

"I just don't get it. Nearly a decade he's been with me. How could she take him away so easily? Like the bar meant nothing to him. Like *I* meant nothing to him," I spoke through my clenched teeth and jerky movements as I turned down my side of the bed and got in.

"You are so clueless as to the power you possess

over people, men especially."

He kissed my head and pulled me in under his arm against his chest.

"What are you going on about? What powers do I *possess*?" I snickered, totally not amused.

"Ever think it was because you did mean so much to him. You found your happiness and now he's going to find his?"

"Working for her won't make him happy. He's happy at the bar. I mean he was all those years. I know I haven't been there much the last six, seven months but still…it's not like anything changed except my presence," I said plucking a rogue feather from the comforter.

Damn, you poke me when I sleep and you hurt. You were way too much money to throw away. I'll live with you poking me until I pluck you to death, evil comforter.

I yanked it out and twirled the tiny feather between my fingers.

"Exactly," he responded.

"Seriously…I don't feel like talking in Morse fucking code. Out with it," I said solemnly.

"You moved on so now it was his time to move on."

"What? Because I found the love of my life and have a family, means I moved on. I haven't moved on. I love that place." I sounded like I was trying to convince myself and Nathan picked up on it immediately.

"I know you do…but hear me out. Okay?" He pulled his head back and lifted my chin to look at him.

"What if, he was waiting around for something he had hoped would come along, and then he realized it would never happen, so he decided cutting ties would be best for everyone? Especially for him. You're gone. Rachel is running the place but she'll leave eventually, too. What's going to be left for him? The new management? Besides...I'm pretty sure you're the only reason he stayed around this long. He wanted to see if we would work out. You think he was just making extra special nice-nice with you while I was blanked out for my sake? No, Jordie. He did it for you. He's loved you for a very long time."

I sat silent for a moment blinking at him and then I laughed.

"You think what? You think he's in *love*? With *me?*" I questioned. "That's absurd, baby."

I adjusted the blanket and my pillows.

Stop adjusting. He knows that's your nervous tick, stupid.

I stopped fidgeting and fixing. Then Nathan began to laugh.

"You know I'm right." He took my hand and kissed it.

"I hate you." I nudged him.

"I hate you too, gorgeous." He leaned over and kissed me.

"Can you do me a favor? Can you check on the kids while I call Rachel and tell her what's going on?" I asked when we came up for air.

Rachel was pretty pissed when she heard the news about Mike. I skipped the part where Nathan thought he left because he was in love with me. She had a complete shit fit when she realized she'd have to interview people again, let alone big brutes as she called them. I reassured her she wouldn't have to and I'd handle it. She was stressed enough with the whole Tyler is cheating crap. After next weekend, she'd be 'I need to plan a wedding in four point two days' stressed. After we hung up, I gave Frank a quick text asking if he knew of any guys looking to moonlight, and of course he did. That man had saved my ass so many times.

I guessed Nathan worked up an appetite because I heard him scrounging around in the kitchen.

"Could he be any louder? Jesus Christ, he's clankin' around in there like a damn bull in a china shop," I muttered to myself as the sound of multiple things crashed to the floor.

"That wasn't a challenge Nathan," I huffed.

I knew he'd be a few minutes so I hopped on my laptop to check out the latest and greatest in the life of Nordie. I did my normal scroll, laugh, click, then wtf is this? Laugh even harder...read some more comments...check out the funny as hell memes until that was I came across a post that caught my attention.

"Fan pic of Bristol and head bouncer at 'The Post' leaving Nordie's apartment."

I clicked on it and scrolled through the normal comments of speculation and outrageousness. The last comment caught my eye. Ol' bitch face was at it again, except this time she wasn't shit slinging. This was true, well half-true.

"Bristol snags another important man out of Jordie's life." I read it out loud, and I could feel my face tightening I was so pissed.

I scrolled further down to read the caption on the picture.

"I was eating dinner when I couldn't help but notice Bristol being seated next to us. I won't even play, I fan-girled for a moment but remained cool. She was with Jordie's head bouncer, Mike! After they ordered their drinks, I overheard him saying to her that she should have let him at least give two weeks notice. And Bristol was kind of...no she was, bitchy to him saying she wasn't going to have him waste two more weeks of his life being Jordie's lap dog. I was sort of shocked because I always had gotten the impression she was so nice. I guess she made him feel bad because he didn't really say anything else the rest of the meal. Bristol was on her phone...a lot. After all that shit, I think she's rude." There were several comments below taking Bristol's side and saying how stressed she must be, blah blah blah.

Okay, so yeah. It was pretty fucking disturbing to me that these women were sticking up for Bristol, especially with her asshole attitude out towards Mike, which I wasn't too thrilled about either. But what really bothered me was that someone just posted this shit...our personal business as if it was *their* personal business. I know I get it, when you're a celebrity or marry one, your privacy goes buh bye, but I hadn't even had the chance to process this shit yet. Why? Why are these women so mean? It's not like I'm some super raunchy chick dry humping guys on a dirt road behind my husband's back. Nathan and me, we're happy. I make him happy, he makes me happy, so I just don't get the whole 'they know what's going on in our lives' thing.

CHAPTER 16

By the time Wednesday rolled around, I was hoping it was Saturday. I had so much going on at once, it was ridiculous. Luckily, Frank had two guys that could work a few weeks until I found permanent replacements. I told him I only needed one but he insisted I have a backup…about fifteen times. Like I should have had all along. I *did* have extra guys working but none of them really worked out too well, and now I was down to four. So, once again Frank was right, I'd put all my eggs in the Mike, Carlos and two guys I barely knew security basket. I was an idiot to think they'd stay there forever.

I guess it was my own selfish self, holding on to some piece of my old life. Something that hadn't changed overnight, but changed anyway, and bam, changed one more time. I knew everything was different. It was a good different of course, but nonetheless, different.

I called the staffing agency and put in a request for applications. Long gone were the days of classifieds in the paper, besides I couldn't trust just any damn person those days.

Everyone wanted a piece of Nathan and me. Whether it was a pic of him and me walking, driving or sitting watching fucking paint dry...they wanted it. The pics of Bristol and Mike leaving our building, followed by the spectacular narrative that twat-a-riffic Deloony posted on Nate-Nation rumors, were flying everywhere. Which I thought was bad enough all by itself, but what bothered me more was that Deloony was in the New York area somewhere and knew where we lived, apparently. I hoped the staffing agency knew how to weed out the blood sucking big mouths and find the proper person for the job.

When Nathan got home, he and Evelyn headed to his office to discuss his plans for Monday. Nathan had to leave and go to Vancouver for a meeting but would be back in two days.

"What was the point of having that extravagant meeting room if you still have to leave us to go to meetings?" I leaned against the doorjamb and pouted.

"Right?" Evelyn asked not taking her eyes off the computer screen.

"I have to be there for this. They have some Swiss GC'rs coming in to fit me for the suits I'll be filming in and other stuff. Lots of wires and latex." He wiggled his eyebrows at me.

"Latex, huh?" I grinned.

Evelyn looked up, gave a small laugh, and shook her head.

"What?" I asked her as I moved to stand next to Nathan.

"Nothing. You guys are cute. It's like a perpetual state of honeymoon with you two," she said as she typed what sounded like a million words a minute.

When she stopped, both Nathan and my phones

dinged at the same time.

"That's all the info you'll need for your trip. Itinerary, flight, hotel, and daily schedules. Obviously, I sent it to both of you," Evelyn said as she stood up.

"Okay, I'm headed down to get Emma."

I grabbed my sweater and put my boots on.

I was a few minutes early so I took a seat on the bench to wait.

"Good afternoon, Mrs. Harper," Joseph the older doorman greeted me and tipped his hat.

"Afternoon." I smiled.

He never spoke to me unless it was hello or goodbye. Frank must have really made an impression.

It was a gorgeous day, and I watched the people walk by, strolling and talking, texting as they made their way down the street. One guy nearly ran into a hot dog cart because he wasn't paying attention. I rolled my eyes at the state of life in the big city.

I saw Emma's car pull up and I stood. She got out and took not even three steps when her books started to fall out of her open backpack.

"This stupid thing," Emma grumbled through her teeth in frustration.

"Hey honey." I bent down to help her pick them up. "Looks like you need a new one of these. We can go shopping for one in a little while," I told her.

"Thanks," she said and stood up when the last of them were safely in the pack.

As I straightened, I saw a black SUV pull to the curb. We began to walk towards the building when I heard my name called. When I glanced around, I immediately wished I hadn't.

"Bristol," I mumbled in annoyance.

"Oh snap. Mom, look it's Bristol Santana. She's

calling you. You know her?" Emma looked baffled by this.

"Yes, I know her," I said through tight lips as I tried to sound civil.

"Jordie, I'm so glad I caught you, and who is this beautiful girl? Wow, she is the spitting image of you Jordan." Bristol smiled at Emma.

"I'm Emma. It's *so* awesome to meet you. Are you here to see Nathan? Are you two doing a movie together?" Emma shot off the questions at rapid-fire speed.

"It's so nice to meet you Emma. I'm Bristol. And no, I've no plans of working with Nathan yet, but I stopped by to see your mom."

Bristol smiled her patronizing bitch smile at Emma, and I wanted to smack it off her mug.

"Jordie, I wanted to give you this," Bristol said handing me a long flat box.

"What is it?" I stared at her blankly without putting out my hand to take it.

"Open it." She paused, then pushed it towards me. "Please." Bristol added that plea with a sarcastic smirk.

I accepted it and opened the card that was with it.

The card read:

Jordie, I'm sure your situation has been stressful. Please, take a day to relax. On me, and bring a friend.

Bristol

"What is it mom?" Emma asked all wide-eyed with excitement.

UGH.

"It's a spa day, Emma, at the Gardens," Bristol answered for me.

"I'm on my way there now, if you'd like to join me.

In fact, my eleven-year-old niece will be with me. They're in from Texas visiting."

"Oh no, I can't now, we have…"

"We have what? I have nothing to do. My homework's all done. Come on, Mom, please?" Emma interrupted whining and begging.

"I can't, sweetie, I have too much to do today."

"I can take her with me, Jordie. If you want?" Bristol smiled vindictively sweet.

This bitch was out for blood. Is she trying to play my kid as a pawn?

"Bristol, I don't know you well enough…" I started but she waved her hand, and the driver side door opened to the SUV.

"But you know him well enough, don't you?" Bristol asked…with a purpose.

"Mike," Emma shouted, and ran over to him as he stepped up the curb.

"Heeeeey kiddo," Mike said as he scooped her up for a hug.

"Be careful, you don't want to wrinkle his shiny new suit," I scoffed.

"Jordie, you really should reconsider my gift. You seem…tense," Bristol said.

Now, at that very moment, I wanted to rip her fucking face off and make her wipe her own ass with it but that wasn't an option, obviously. Suddenly, a crowd of voices broke apart my daydream of tearing her apart limb for limb.

Fucking paps.

"Please Mom. I'll be fine. Pleaaaseeeee?" Emma begged.

"C'mon Jords. I haven't seen the kid in a while. You know I'll take care of her," Mike pleaded on Emma's behalf in a somber voice.

"Okay, but what time do you expect to be back? She isn't on vacation like your niece. She has school tomorrow," I asked letting my defensive wall down.

After all, it was still Mike. Just Mike in a Prada suit.

"Around seven, I'd say, eight at the latest. We'll be eating dinner at The Tavern afterwards, so it just depends on how dinner goes," Bristol said smiling down at Emma the whole time.

"Give me your bag," I said reluctantly to Emma. "Behave yourself. Remember someone is *always* watching. As you can see…" I threw my hand in the air to point out all the clickers.

Fucking savages.

"Thanks Mom." Emma hugged me and grabbed Mike's hand.

"I'll bring her up when we get back," Mike assured me as he walked her to the truck.

"You'd better." I gave a tight thin-lipped smile.

"So good to see you again, Jordie." Bristol smiled.

"I do hope you use that." She nodded towards the spa day gift card.

"Thanks," was all I said, as I watched Emma buckle up and wave goodbye to me.

By the time I got back to our apartment, I had cursed so much that I undoubtedly made up words because I ran out, and if twat-loaf wasn't a word before it sure as hell was after my elevator ride.

"She is such an asshole bitch," I screamed as I walked in, slamming the door before I double fisted my hair in frustration.

"What? Who? Jordie, are you okay? Jesus, you're gunna' pull your hair out, Mija, stop;" Evelyn said to me as she took my hands in hers.

"Whats wrong?" Nathan came running in from down the hall. "That mother fucking bitch asshole, Bristol, *that's* what's wrong."

I went through what happened with them, and I could see Evelyn getting more and more agitated as the story played out.

"I'll call her and get her to bring Emma back." Evelyn pulled out her cell but I stopped her.

"No, its fine. It will just be a letdown to Emma, at this point. She hasn't seen Mike in forever and the seed's been planted so she's excited to spend time with Briiistol." I made a sour grapes face while I mocked her name.

"Evelyn, you can go," Nathan said and put his arms around me.

I think he knew I was about to cry.

"Okay," she said slowly. "Are you sure, Jordie? I don't mind. I'll be the bad guy."

"It's fine. Thank you. I appreciate it." I walked over and gave her a hug.

"See you tomorrow." I sniffled and turned towards the bedrooms to get Nate up from his nap. I heard him stirring in his crib through the monitor.

Thursday was relatively quiet. I spoke with Rachel. Everything was set up for us to be at The London in Midtown at nine sharp for the big engagement extravaganza. I received specific instructions that this was to be in 'Real-time' and not Jordie and Rachel time. Nine PM sharp it was.

While Nathan was finishing up in the media room, I went to check on the kids before getting myself settled for the night. After, I took a seat on the chaise to check my email and stuff. I decided to skip Nate-Nation because I couldn't handle Deloony and her sheep tonight. Honestly, I was sort of over it all. There was no good reason to acknowledge it anymore. I knew our family was secure, and Nathan and I were better than good. Instead, I decided to read what was important.

August 23rd

I've ridden my bike around that neighborhood every night this past week. I KNOW there's something. I feel obsessed. But, you need something to be obsessed with, right? Only, I don't have anything...

August 30th

I walked up and down the block tonight. Back and forth, and I blended in. It's amazing how many people wear Yankee caps and sunglasses at night. Suddenly, I got bits and pieces. Flashes of those boots. I see them and someone's hands with blood on them. Jesus Christ, did I hurt someone? Did I like help a murderer? No...not enough blood for that. But, those hands. I CANT FUCKING EXPLAIN IT. I never thought that to get my memories back I'd have to lose my goddamned mind like this. I need a break. But I can't stop thinking about it. Any of it.

I should call Lena. Maybe get some. Did I really just say that? I guess so. Maybe a stress reliever is all I need to get focused again.

I stared straight ahead and closed the journal.

Maybe I should get some?

I felt my stomach tighten up and my teeth clenched.

Quit being such a drama mamma. He didn't know you existed, but then again even when he didn't know, he knew. Keep reading.

I opened it the book again, and took a deep breath in, and held it for a few seconds, before letting it out with a big gush of air and noise. At the same time, Nathan walked in the room and smiled at me.

"What are you smiling at, ya nut-job?" I asked with a grin.

"Just the fact that you thought you couldn't deal

with knowing and now you're in here doing some light reading without me."

Nathan jumped on the bed, laid back against the pillows and motioned me to come sit with him. He sat up against the headboard and I sat in between his legs leaning my back on his chest. He rested his chin on my shoulder for a second and then kissed it.

August 31st

I made plans with Lena for next week. I rented a room on a different floor. The folks will be back. I don't want to disappoint Mom by looking like a womanizer, but goddamn, I was willing to try anything at this point. Even no strings attached sex. I have no idea if that is the norm for me even. Maybe I should ask Frank or Tyler.

September 3rd

I asked Frank if I was a no strings attached one night stander kind of guy, or what....His response was 'or what'. Instead of answers, I'm ending up with more questions.

September 16th

Now I know I'm fucking mental. What kind of man has a hot chick rubbing all up on him begging for it...and he says no? It was like a bad trip. At first, I was ok, I was into it. Alright, yeah she's hot. I'm a guy...I got shot and can't remember anything so I deserve a little right? WRONG. The only thing that got fucked was my mind. One. Huge. Mind Fuck. I was fine, doing the over the clothes shit, but once her shirt came off, and she straddled me, my brain hurt. I literally shook my head to try to shake it off...but I couldn't. The more she moved the more flashed through my mind. Holy fuck just thinking about it exhausts me. It was tolerable until she put her hands in my hair. Then it was like I was being haunted by my own memory. A voice, it was HER voice, repeating my name. Nathan. Nathan. Nathan. I practically tossed Lena off me. I apologized and told her she had to go. The boots. The hands. The voice were all connected...but who is she?

I closed the journal and realized I had a steady stream of tears running down my face. I felt like I was going to puke. I ripped Nathan's hands apart from around me and literally jumped out of the bed, and ran to the bathroom.

I was sweaty and clammy.

What. The. Fuck. How much of the 'over the clothes thing' did he do with her? She was a hot chick rubbing all up against him? Jordan, you stupid, stupid, stupid ass. You knew this was coming.

"Jordan? Unlock the door," Nathan called through the door but I made no attempt to move.

"Please?" he asked.

Still, I leaned against the vanity sink, wiping my tears.

"Now..." Nathan demanded.

Fuck. He means business.

I walked over and unlocked the door.

"If you "knew" there was something missing, someone important, something you were obsessing over, why would you do *that*?" I broke down.

I wasn't expecting that. I didn't even know how I felt about him knowing that was in there and thinking it was okay for me to read it. And with *her*? He knew how I felt about her. What's worse was she knew about me and never mentioned it. She isn't one of those bitches that worry about other people's needs. If she thought telling him about me, Emma, and the baby would benefit her, she'd have been all over it.

Another bitch. What is wrong with these women?

"I'm not okay with *that*, Nathan," I sobbed. "I need to know if there is more of *that*? If so, I'm out. I'm not reading anymore."

I wrapped my arms around my stomach and bent over crying harder. Silently, but harder.

"No more. That was the last time I touched anyone," Nathan answered.

I stood up, wiped my tears, and sniffled.

"That broke my heart, Nathan."

I started to cry again but held it back a bit. If I hadn't, I would have gone into full on 'ugly cry', and I wasn't having that shit.

Nathan pushed the hair away from my face and hugged me.

"Mine too, baby. I didn't even know you existed yet I was heartbroken and disgusted with myself." He kissed the top of my head then picked me up so I could sit on the counter.

"I love you that much, Jordan. I'm so sorry."

He leaned in and kissed me. Not his, I wanna eat your face and hump you until you can't stand kind of kiss, either. It was a sweet long and apologetic kiss.

"You're forgiven." I sniffled, and wrapped my legs around him.

Blue eyes to green, we searched each other's souls.

"I can't forgive myself, and I sure as hell don't expect you to forgive me that quickly," Nathan joked and rested his forehead against mine.

"I won't apologize for how I feel, but I can forgive you. I'll just keep telling myself you were out of your mind." I grinned.

"This is why I wanted to do this with you. Why I wanted you to read this," Nathan said.

"So we would fight and make up?" I leaned in and

kissed him.

"No. I didn't want any secrets between us. I didn't want to feel like I was hiding it from you. I wanted you to know so we could move past it, together. I couldn't forgive myself without knowing you forgave me," he confessed.

"Well, go easy on yourself. We'll get through this," I said as I pulled my shirt over my head.

"Oh yeah, and how will we manage that?" he asked with his gorgeous lazy grin that made me want to bite his lip and do dirty, dirty things to him.

"Lots and lots of this." I pulled him as close as possible and my hands were in his hair a second later. I forgave him in my own special way, over and over, that night.

CHAPTER 17

I ran around all day Friday. Evelyn came with me because Nathan had gone with Tyler to pick up his mom and siblings at the airport and get them settled. I had to keep Rachel busy so we met her at the Bar. Fiona came along with us as well. I was happy because it meant I got to spend a good part of the day with my little handsome man before he went to G Ma's for the weekend. Emma was going to Kelly's after school so we had a few hours before I had to be back to get her ready to go, and my sister wasn't good with the whole waiting thing.

We went to a few shops until Rachel and I picked out two perfect dresses for our "Girls Night Out" dinner. I just had to get her there at nine and all would be right with the world.

When we pulled up to her place, I hugged her, and handed her the dress bag.

"Such a hot dress," I said.

"Too bad you're the only one that's going to see it." She sulked.

"Just leave it on for when he gets home." I tried to cheer her up.

"Yeah. I guess." She pulled her keys out of her purse.

"Rach, I promise you, he isn't steppin' out on you. I'll be here at eight-forty. Got it? We cannot be late. We'll lose the reservation. Chin up until then. No frowny faces allowed." I reached over and pushed her cheeks up into a smile like putty in my hands but she stood there deadpanning me.

"You're an asshole," she said through me holding her lips up.

I busted out laughing and let go when I felt her mouth tighten into a smile.

"There we go. Much better." I sat back in the driver's seat.

She flipped me the finger and gave me the international duck face of fuck off.

"Okay, biotch. See you later. Bye Fiona. It was nice to see you and thank you for that seminar on ovulation and hormones. I'll pick up my pamphlets at the door," she shouted into the back to Nathan's mom with a smile and a humorous eye roll.

"Yeah yeah smart ass," Fiona replied and made an air kiss sound.

Evelyn hopped out here, too, because it was a block away from the subway station.

"Goodbye. Go. Behave and have fun tonight." She shoo'd Rachel off.

"Bye, Ev, see you Monday. Bye, Rach, see you in a few hours."

Joseph greeted me at the curb when I pulled up and removed the bags from the back of my truck. The younger kid helped Fiona out, taking her hand so she'd keep her footing because my truck was a bit high for her.

"Thank you, sweetheart," she said to him before getting Nate out.

Nathan's town car arrived at the curb as Joseph walked around with all our crap.

"I'll get that, Joseph. Thank you." I reached for the dress bag.

"Don't be silly, Mrs. Harper. Frank gave me permission to help today." He winked and let out a small laugh.

I laughed with him because he would always help me out even when Frank would get all cranky pants on him.

Nathan came over, took Nate from his mother, and gave her a kiss.

"Is he all packed, Jordan?" she asked while adjusting Nate's jacket.

"Yepp, just gotta' go get it," I answered as we walked to the elevator.

Nathan held Nate in one arm and my hand with the other. My sister got there a few minutes before Emma got home so I decided to show her my dress and Nathan's finished media room.

"Fancy," she said, and whistled when she saw the room.

"Whatever."

I laughed as we headed to my bedroom when I heard Emma come in. She talked with Nathan while I showed Kelly my dress. When we got back out to the living room, she wasn't there.

"Where'd Emma go?" I asked Nathan.

"In her room I guess." He shrugged.

I went down to her room. The door wasn't open so I knocked lightly before I went in. As I stood in her doorway, she came out of her bathroom. She stood there stunned for a second then ran back in the bathroom. I was definitely going to lose my shit.

"Emma Lynn Harper, get your ass out here right now," I yelled at her.

"I will in a second," she responded through the closed door. I tried to open it but she'd locked it.

"Emma, I will bust this door down if I have to ask again," I shouted through the crack.

"No way," she yelled back.

By that time, Kelly and Nathan had come down to see what the hell was going on. They stood in the doorway staring at me like I was nuts.

"I'm going to kill this kid. She knowingly went against what I said." I kicked the door. "Get out here," I said through clenched teeth.

"Open the door, here is a pair of shorts." I grabbed the pair she had on the bed.

When she came out, her face was red and she was sniffling. She'd obviously been crying. Whereas, I was sure my face was red from fury.

Kelly and Nathan stood there quiet, still trying to figure out what was going on when my next words probably solved the mystery.

"What did I tell you about shaving your legs?" I yelled. "Emma you're ten."

Nathan and Kelly both made the 'ooh' face and left the room.

"You said I couldn't shave my legs," she snapped back at me.

"I did say that…so why do your legs appear to be shaved?"

"I didn't shave them. They were waxed."

I had never hit Emma. I don't think violence is the answer to fixing an attitude but at that moment, it was *really* hard not to slap her across the mouth for her attitude and disrespect.

"What do you mean they were waxed? When the hell did this happ..." I stopped and then it smacked me in the face like a big ol' tuna tail.

"That Bitttch," I screamed.

Suddenly Emma's waxed legs were the least of my concerns. Poor kid did have pretty hairy legs, so she would do it eventually anyway, but now I was on a whole new tangent.

"Nathan. Nathan," I yelled.

"Yeah?" He sounded unsure as he poked his head in.

"Get Bristol on the phone...now," I seethed.

My sister came back in and sat on the bed.

"Jordan, I have to confess. I was going to teach her how to shave this weekend. C'mon. What would you have done if Mom forbade you from shaving those hairy ass legs of yours? You would have said, eff off, and done it right in front of her." She smiled.

I knew she was right.

"Damn, she just seems way too young to start all that. She's ten. Yes, she acts like she's older but she's still only ten. She's my baby Kelly," I pouted.

"No, your baby is Nate. Your young lady is Emma," she corrected me.

"Still, that bitch Bristol is going to hear it from me." I stood up.

"Why Jordan? It's exactly what she wants," Nathan said, leaning against the doorjamb.

"No, what she wants is you. She's played her little head trips with me all along and that was fine...but now...my kid is involved. Fuck that." I stomped out of the room.

"Emma Lynn, where are you?" I called for her.

"Here Mom." Her voice came from behind me.

"Look, your disrespect for me lately has got to stop here. I will deal with this whole defying me thing when you get home Sunday. Right now I'm way too hot to even think about discussing it." I pulled her in and hugged her.

"Mom."

"Yeah sweetie."

"That waxing thing…"

"What about it?"

"It's been a day and it still hurts," she whined.

I let out a small laugh and looked down at her.

"Put some aloe on it when you get to Aunt Kelly's." I kissed the top of her head.

Bristol…You better run, bitch.

Nathan left at six to pick up Tyler and his family. They had to stop by the jewelry store to pick up the ring because Tyler had nowhere safe to hide it. Rachel had her hands all over the place. The bar, their apartment, or our place, nothing was safe. She was always digging through something of mine.

I was in the bathroom straightening my hair when I got a text from Mike asking how I was. I ignored it. I couldn't deal with that shit right then. Anything that remotely reminded me of Bristol, I wanted to throw under a moving bus. That woman had some nerve.

When I finished my hair, I changed into my just above the knee length capped sleeve, black sequin top, black tulle bottom dress, and slipped on my very first pair of Valentino Garavani's. Fresh off the plane from Paris, France this afternoon. I was ashamed of myself for spending what I had on them. I could get twenty pairs of boots for what I spent on this one pair of shoes but it was for a special occasion, so I splurged.

As I walked down the hallway, I laughed at the

clickety-clack sound they made. I wasn't used to hearing that sound from underneath me. I also wasn't used to being so tall. I was holding my sapphire necklace in one hand and my black matching clutch in the other. When I got to the living room, Frank was on the couch reading a paper.

"They still make them things?" I joked about his newspaper.

"Looks that way. I know I was surprised as well." He laughed as he folded it up and put it on the table.

"Look at you. You look beautiful Jordan." He reached for my hand and gave me a twirl.

"Thank you sir." I curtsied. "Could I trouble you to put this on me please?"

I held out my hand and showed him my necklace. He took it from me and I moved my hair out of the way. My phone began to ring in my clutch. I reached in to get it but when I saw it was Mike, I bumped his call and put it away.

"Ready to go?" Frank asked.

"Ready."

We arrived at The London at nine sharp, just like I was instructed. When Frank took the ticket from the valet, Rachel gave me a wtf look.

"The pitbull is joining us for our girl's night out?" she snorted.

"Ha!" I busted out and looked back at Frank.

"I'm not a pitbull," he replied in a sort of sing songy voice.

"No, you're a bat with that fucking hearing..." Rachel mumbled and we all laughed.

I had no idea where they were so when the host led us through the main dining area I made sure I stayed in front of Rachel so she wouldn't see everyone and ruin the surprise. As we neared the back, I saw there was a semi-private area.

"Jesus Christ where are we sitting? In the kitchen, buddy?" Rachel blurted out.

I smacked her with my clutch by waving my arm behind me.

"Be nice Rachel," I hissed.

Just as we got to the entrance of the room, I stepped to the side so she could walk in first. I looked in and saw my gorgeous husband in that Gucci suit that makes me drippy in all the right places.

Rachel blurted, "What are we getting our own—"

She stopped dead in her tracks when she realized who was in the room.

"What...the...hell? It isn't my birthday. Is it?" She looked at me dumbfounded.

All I could do was laugh because it was a rare thing to see Rachel speechless. It was like seeing a 'unicorn shitting another unicorn who was shitting a rainbow' kind of rare.

When the lights dimmed, I nodded for her to look across the room at where Tyler was sitting up on a make shift stage area. He was sitting on a stool with a slide show of pictures running on a wall behind him.

Nathan came and stood next to me. I started to get all teary-eyed when I saw Rachel's eyes fill up as she made her way to Tyler. He began to play his guitar and sing a song he wrote for her. Nathan slipped his arm around my waist and kissed my head.

"You look amazing," he whispered in my ear.

"You are one hot piece of ass, Mister Harper, and I can't wait to take that suit off of you," I whispered back.

"Really, now. I may have some fun myself taking that dress off of you...with my teeth." He ran his hand over my hips and over my ass. I sucked in a huge breath and held it because his hand was so close to hem of my dress.

"You have any idea how easily my hand could disappear up here and nobody would be the wiser with all this fluffy stuff to work under." He positioned me so I was standing in front of him as he hugged me from behind.

I'm pretty sure it was to hide what was happening inside his pants at that moment. I dropped my clutch on purpose, bent over to pick it up, and when I rubbed against him, he let out a hushed groan.

I took a tiny step away from him so the party in his pants would settle down before the lights got turned back up. He moved my hair to the side and kissed my neck.

"Just you wait," he said with his lips pressed against the skin right below my ear.

I just concentrated on breathing or I was going to pass out from all the blood rushing to one place…and it wasn't my head. I felt his phone vibrate as the lights began to come back on and he pulled it out of his pocket. He stifled a laugh.

I looked back at him in question and he turned his phone so I could see what it said.

Wildly inappropriate behavior at an engagement party, FYI

It was from Frank.

Before Nathan turned it away, another text came through but he didn't realize it and put the phone back in his pocket. He began to make his way to where Rachel and Tyler were with me right behind him. Nathan pulled me tight against his side. Tyler was on his knee in front of Rachel.

"Wanna' make an honest man out of me?" He grinned up at her and she knelt down with him, and said yes. Well, she cried yes.

As soon as they finished, she turned and threw her arms around me.

"Is this payback, you effin bitch, for the week I had to keep my mouth shut about your engagement?" She laughed.

"Ohh yeah, I forgot about all that. Yepp, consider us even. I'm so happy for you," I gushed.

"Alright, tone it down, no need to get all period hormonal on me now." She busted out laughing.

"Go meet your new mother-in-law and sibling-in-laws." I glanced over at Tyler.

"When did we decide to grow up, Jordan?" Rachel asked me dead serious.

"I don't think we had any say in this." I smiled. "It was just time, I guess."

I hugged her before she walked away.

"Wanna go find a utility closet or something?" I asked Nathan who was standing behind me again.

"I thought you'd never ask." He smiled and escorted me out of the room.

We looked all over that place, not one room private enough for a quickie, and I don't do bathrooms. *Yuck.* I noticed the line of cars out the front window and I had an idea.

"Is your car service still out there?" I grinned mischievously at him.

"You're brilliant," he said as he led the way.

When we got out front, we stopped while Nathan looked for the driver. I looked the opposite way to where I noticed Mike sitting in a black SUV.

"That bitch is *here?*" I said overly loud, gaining the attention of quite a few people in close proximity to me, including Mike.

"Jordie," Mike called from the truck as he got out.

As he got closer, I turned my back to him and

Nathan finally realized what was going on.

"Jordie, talk to me. Please? I texted you earlier."

"I have nothing to say to *Michael.*" I pulled Nathan with me as I walked away.

"Talk about a cock block," Nathan muttered.

As we approached the door to go back inside, Bristol was on her way out. She was doing something on her phone so I thought we got lucky when she didn't look up. Although, I wouldn't have minded since I wanted to rip her head off and feed it to her ass for breakfast. After all, she had paid to have my ten year old's legs waxed.

Bigger person, Jordan...be the bigger person. I chose not to fight that battle.

"Jordie? Nate? What a coincidence bumping into you here,." Bristol said just as we slipped past her.

God dammit.

"Sorry, can't talk. Need to get back inside. Nice to see you," I said in one swift sentence.

"Jordie, could I steal you for a second? I'd really like to clear something up with you." She put on one hell of a dog and pony show when people were watching.

"I'm going to say goodbye to everyone, let them know you aren't feeling well, and grab my jacket." Nathan kissed my forehead and quietly asked if I was okay. I nodded and let his hand go.

"Tell Rachel I'll call her tomorrow," I told him and then turned to Bristol.

"What can I do for you Bristol?"

As if my less than enthusiastic tone wasn't evident enough, my lack of posture and eye contact should have gotten the message across loud and clear. I didn't want any part of this.

"Jordie, I know the things that you see on the Internet must really get to you, but I want you to know that I would never, ever go after a married man." She put her hand on mine. But when, she did this weird puppy dog, sympathetic pity thing with her eyes, it made me snap.

"Well that's reassuring, being that you were like a rabid dog snatching up a man that was already employed…just to fuck me. But, unlike *Michael*, I know *my husband* has no reason to stray. He fought pretty damn hard to find me so I'm pretty sure he isn't going anywhere, not that I need to tell you that, right? You'd *never* go after someone's husband," I smiled sweetly and spoke softly.

It's more threatening when you whisper and have a calm beady eye stare going on. That's right. I busted out the Ol' crazy eyes trick. Besides, the paps were everywhere now so to them we were just having a friendly conversation.

"Bristol, Jordie, can we get a pic of you two?" one of the paps asked.

"Well you sure can." I smiled animatedly and looked at Bristol. "Right, friend?"

I pulled her in close to me with my arm around her shoulder and smiled for the cameras.

"Right, friend," Bristol answered through clenched teeth.

Nathan walked out of the restaurant with Rachel and Tyler in tow. The three of them stood at the door frozen with an amused look on their faces. I noticed Nathan's eyes look past behind me for a second but by the time I turned around there were just a few people crossing the street. When I looked back, he smiled. Not a normal Nathan smile. Something was up. Before we parted ways, Bristol and I laid on the theatrics by embracing in a long sisterly hug and lots of smiles. We said our goodbyes and hopped in the limo.

CHAPTER 18

October 3rd

That night with Lena caused something in my brain to snap. I don't give a shit what happened to me in the past. All I can think about is HER!!!

Night after night, I ride my bike out to the East Village and watch everyone go by. Even the sky holds some sort of importance in the grand scheme of it all, but I can't put it together. So I wander.

October 21st

Yesterday I got there early, so I took a seat on a bench. It was dusk so I could still see faces. Around 5, I noticed Tyler and Rachel walking across the street. I stood to call them but I saw they had a little girl with them. I walked a little behind them on the opposite side of the street. When I saw the bar, I assumed it was where Rachel works. I knew she was a bartender, I just didn't know where. But they didn't go to the bar. They stopped at the building next to it. I looked up and saw lights on. They went inside. I looked higher...to the sky above that building...it sucker punched me. I KNOW that sky.

October 23rd

I stayed in and watched TV all day. Flipping through the channels, I came across an older movie with Melissa Joan Hart and the guy from Entourage...Grenier...I stayed on it for a few seconds because Ali Larter looked amazing with red hair but then a song began playing and the hair on my neck stood up. I KNEW the song. My heart broke...it actually drew my body inward. GODDAMN IT, WHY CANT I REMEMBER ANY OF THIS??? WHAT AM I DOING WRONG? I cried...alone...on the couch of the hotel...with a bag of Cheetos. I just cried.

"I'll never be able to watch you eat Cheetos again." I closed the journal with a quick snap and put it on my nightstand.

"Well, I hope you never watch me eat anything...ever, honestly. That's sort of strange." We laughed together, then he continued. "Yeah, that was a rough night for me. You have no idea how frustrating it is to want something so bad and not even know what it is."

He ran his hand over my stomach with his flattened hand.

Stop that, you're making me tingle.

"It's that feeling when the answer is riiiight there on the tip of your tongue but never evolves into an answer." He rolled onto his side. He had his one arm across his chest with his hand tucked under the other arm. He was rubbing my stomach still and his facial expression read concentration.

"You okay?" I asked but he was silent.

"Seriously, Nathan. What is it?"

"I was just thinking about something Lena said to

me that night. It didn't make any sense then, but it does now. Wow, she's such a bitch," he said with a sneer.

"Not exactly who I'd like to hear you're thinking about, but okay, I'll play. What did she say?" I asked sarcastically.

"She said it was ironic that I was the one throwing her out because she was willing to accept me all fucked up, just the way I was. Even if I got my memory back, and lost me, she'd still be willing to take that chance just to be with me. Unlike those who have the chance to claim what's theirs but instead choose not to. They have no idea what they're giving up. Those who don't want to know what they've thrown away. I get it now."

"Talk about obsessed." I sneered.

"Isn't it amazing that even though I had the memory of an Alzheimer's patient, I still knew it was wrong. That she wasn't you. You were missing." He propped himself up and gave the side of my panties a snap.

"Yeah, that's some Nicolas Sparks, *The Notebook*, shit right there," I said, clearly not enjoying the thought of that intimate incident.

He leaned over and kissed my stomach.

Ooh my ohh my...

As he kissed and touched me, he made his way to where he hovered over me between my legs.

"You...know...I..." Well, fuck I can't think.

"You what?" He asked between his kisses that became more and more sensual with each one.

"I...I don't know."

I gave up exasperated and grabbed his hair with both hands. He let out one of his panty dropping growls and I was done. I forgot about all of it. The shitty night, Bristol, and the fact that something was bothering Nathan and I had no idea what. All I could feel was his breath against my skin and his tongue never leaving my body as he tugged my panties off. His kisses trailed down and stopped right before his final destination. Then he wrapped his arms under my knees, grabbed the top of my thighs, and yanked me down so I went from leaning against the headboard to flat on my back. His hand was back on my stomach as he made his way up my shirt while his mouth made its way down. It was going to be one of those amazing I see colors and fireworks kind of night.

I woke up sweating around two thirty in the morning. I looked over and Nathan had me tucked under him. His one hand was above him and in my hair, his other hand was still holding one of my breasts, which made me stifle a laugh, and his leg was across mine. Literally, he had half his body draped over me. No wonder I was sweating.

I gently lifted his hand off my chest and started to wriggle out from under him. He mumbled a little bit and rolled over freeing me from my own personal sauna. As I slipped on my shirt, I heard his phone vibrate. I ignored it, of course, because I wasn't a snooper. I knew there was nothing but pics of us, the kids, and the family, some famous names and numbers but I wasn't interested in that stuff anyway.

I went pee and when I came back, it buzzed again. I went over and clicked it off so it would stop and headed out to get a drink. When I came back in, I stood at the floor to ceiling window and looked out over the city. I loved the privacy glass option. We could always see out but nobody could see in. Even at quarter to three in the morning, it was bustling out there.

I heard rustling in the sheets but paid no mind to it until I felt him against me from behind. He slid his hands around, and rubbed back and forth over my rib cage, massaging me. I raised my arm over my head so I could touch his hair. He found the spot in the crook of my neck and walked us to the window.

Score...Finally, window sex!

The thought alone made my legs weak. Knowing all that was keeping the entire Upper East Side from seeing us was some window tint, pretty much made me shameless.

Once we were at the window, he pressed up against me as his hand found his way down to me. The window was cold and being up against it so hard made every nerve tingle.

He hasn't even touched you there yet...Jesus Christ, this man.

It didn't matter that he was simply groping me he did it for me. The thought of Nathan's hands touching every inch of my skin, biting me playfully and growling just the right things in my ear was all I needed. The man was a bucket of sex appeal and he belonged to me.

He slipped two fingers in and moved his thumb just right...once...twice...*fuck...game over.* I came apart...I mean really *came* apart. I must have been talking some pretty dirty shit because Nathan let loose. Now don't get me wrong, he's always a beast in bed. It never mattered if we took our time, fucked like bunnies, or just teased each other; it had always been something special, different, exciting...but when he got like this...when I could tell he wasn't holding back at all, I could expect a few bruises in the morning on the both of us.

He shoved his hand into the hair at the nape of my neck and held it so tight and close that I couldn't really move. He pulled me back away from the window and bent me over.

"Put both hands on the glass," he demanded as he smacked my ass right where he knew I wanted it, between my cheek and thigh. I screamed out in pleasure, which just told him to smack it again.

"Do you even know how much you mean to me?" he asked as he slid his hand between my legs from behind and found my spot. I couldn't answer him...shit...I couldn't form a thought let alone string any words together.

"Do you?" He stopped touching me and nudged into me from behind, hard, pushing me forward a bit.

"I think...I think I do," I answered, slightly dazed.

Can't we discuss this later? Oh god. He's going to end up 'fucking me stupid'.

He nudged me again.

"This is mine."

He reached around and touched me, but this time he may as well have whipped out a flag and claimed it, he was so rough.

"Ye...yes...all...yours. Nathan, *please baby,* do something before I fucking explode," I begged and pushed against him.

That's all it took, me asking him. His long fingers explored me for a few moments until I felt him replace his hand with his dick, rubbing slowly against me.

"Oh my god, Nathan, *please,*" I screamed out, part in pure fucking pleasure and part because I needed him to be inside me.

He grabbed my hips, and yanked me up so hard that my feet left the ground about an inch or so I'd say, while he held me there and pounded into me.

I was wrong...He was going to fuck me into a sex coma. One floor up from fucking me stupid...It's coming.

I lost all control and any sense of reality. With that,

my arms became weak. He stopped, pulled me up, and walked me to the chaise.

"Nathan...I have no strength...two already...I'm..." I peeped out, dropping my head onto the lounger as we knelt down in front of it.

"You want to stop?" He leaned forward, pushed the hair off my face, and kissed my neck.

"No." I shook my head.

"Just don't expect any reverse cowboy action from me." I let out a small laugh.

He kissed my shoulder and stood up, helping me up with him. He walked us over to the bed and told me to lie down. I did what I was told and waited as he climbed over me.

My god, I was a big drippy ball of sexual tension and he knew it.

"I want to feel you come apart around me," he said in my ear.

A few minutes later, I did just that. It was rough and sweet all in one. Then boom, just like that he proved another one of my 'that shit doesn't happen in real life' theories to hell. Four little words and I was done.

"Come for me, Jordan," Nathan said through his clenched teeth and his eyes never leaving mine. "I want to see you, feel you come apart under me."

He begged and I lost it. He never took his eyes off me. I could feel them burn through me, and it wasn't until I was done that he let go.

I slept in Saturday morning. I was so fantastically sore that when I yelped as I stretched and got out of bed, I smiled. I could hear Nathan talking to someone so I decided to hop in the shower and let the hot water work over some of those sore muscles I had. I hit the pre-heat shower button and started to brush my teeth. I hopped in and just let the water wash over me for a good five or ten minutes. The other plus side to the new place...the water never turned cold.

After my ridiculously long shower, I wrapped a towel around my head, dried off, and threw on my favorite pair of sweats and one of my old sweatshirts. It's been a while since I wore anything dressed down like this.

The forecast was calling for snow and the sky looked about right for it. I planned to spend the day watching TV with three of my favorite men. Nathan, and Ben and Jerry. When I headed down the hallway, I heard Nathan still talking. When I passed by, I realized the door was almost all the way shut so I didn't stop. I figured he needed to be alone.

I grabbed some Chunky Monkey out of the Freezer, my favorite blanket off the couch and made myself comfortable. It was the first time using the TV in the new place so it even took me a minute to figure out how to turn it on. Once I did though I was flipping through five hundred channels of crap. I turned E¡ on and kept up with the Kardashians for like three seconds before the mom made me want to gouge my own eyes out with a rusty nail. I had to admit that I love Khloe though. I totally fangirled when Nathan introduced us at a party in LA. I have that picture filed under 'holy shit, did that just happen?'

I began flipping through the channels again when I stopped at 'Old Yeller'. I put down the remote and dug into my Chunky Monkey. Just as the end of the movie was playing my phone rang, it was Emma. I was a sobbing mess when I answered the phone on speaker. I wasn't putting Ben or Jerry down.

"Hey sweetie." I sniffled when I answered.

"Hi Mom. What's wrong? You okay?" She'd picked up on my tone immediately.

"Yeah, baby I'm fine. I just watched Old Yeller," I

explained.

"Oh Christ, not Old Yeller. Who let you watch that, Jordan?" I heard Kelly chime in from the background. I guessed I was on speaker as well.

"Shut up, Kel," I yelled back at her and started sobbing again.

"Mom, it's okay. I promise you, they did what was best for Ol'Yeller," Emma assured me.

"Wow, I step away for an hour, and right away you fall apart. You know it's bad when a ten year old is teaching her mother life lessons," Nathan said as he walked in the living room and sat down next to me.

"Hi Em," he added.

"Hey Nathan," she said.

"I just wanted to let you know that Aunt Kelly said that if it snows there, she isn't bringing me home until Tuesday." She relayed the message.

"Okay. I'd rather you guys stay put if it gets bad out. No driving, tell her. Walk up to the store if you need something. It's like a half a block away."

"Yes mom. Love you. Talk to ya' later. Love you, too, Nathan," Emma said before hanging up.

"Well, I love you, too." I stared at my phone before tossing it on the couch pillow.

"She probably couldn't handle all the weepiness that's happening over here," Nathan said stifling his laugh.

"Fuck off, Nathan." I sniffled playfully as I sat up. I wiped my nose across my sleeve and said "Gimmee a kiss." While making a snot nosed fish face.

"I will, I'll kiss that mouth, I don't care what you have all over it." He leaned in and I pushed him away playfully.

"Ew noooo, you're gross!" I laughed as he kept coming at me.

"I'll take your lips any way I can get them sugar." He tackled me and we fell to the floor. I laughed until I nearly peed in my pants.

Nathan just watched me with a happy smile on his face.

CHAPTER 19

Nathan wanted to take a nap since he pretty much stayed awake after the three am sexapalooza. Something was troubling him. I thought that maybe it was work. He was rather vehement last night when he mentioned not acting anymore. Maybe he would try directing or producing, or perhaps that was just his penis talking. I didn't care what he did as long as we were happy and we can take care of our kids. We laid down together and he fell out almost immediately.

I ran my fingers through his hair as I watched him breathe. He had a full on bear hug around me so I could only move my arms from the elbows down. I was sure I looked comical trying to pick up his journal. I slid myself up carefully, so I didn't wake him, and adjusted myself to get comfortable.

"Let's see what you were thinking next, Mister Harper," I said with a sigh, and opened the book.

October 31st

It's Halloween night, and I sat on the bench. I've watched that building every single night for the last few nights but seen nobody come in, or out- no one but Rachel and Tyler going in with the little girl. I hadn't talked to Tyler much since the whole man whoring comment...why am I lying? I haven't talked to anyone really aside from my parents. Not even Frank. He went home to LA for a few weeks, but he'll be back tomorrow actually.

Things with Mom are much better. She doesn't understand why I have to go out on my bike for hours every night...but she said if it helps clear my head, she understands. I know she worries.

HOLY SHIT. First time in ten days, I've seen someone other than the three of them come or go. A woman...I couldn't make out her face or anything. It's the same kid. She's almost as tall as the small woman, until she jumps off the bottom step dressed in a costume. Looks like they're waiting for someone. I think the woman is pregnant.

They must all been going Trick-or-Treating together, that's cool. I hear the kid yell out Frank's name and I look up just in time to see Frank pick the kid up and hug her. Then he hugs the pregnant girl and gives her a kiss on the cheek. That made my blood boil...why would he lie to me about when he'd be back? But, what really pushed me over the edge was when Mom and Dad got out of Frank's car.

November 1st

I'm pretty sure I got so angry I blacked out.

The last thing I remember was standing up and pacing back and forth, back and forth. I remember hearing the woman laugh and it echoed in my mind. I knew it matched the hands and the boots. I wondered why everyone I cared about was over there. Did I miss a text or a call with an invite? No. They're hiding something. I remember I stopped pacing, and stopped thinking. I decided to go over and find out what the fuck was going on but when I turned, I bumped right into Frank. That's the last thing I remember...so I know a lot more info now. I know everyone is hiding something from me. I feel like they're hiding my happiness. I'm done. Done with all of them. If they want to shut me out, I can do the same to them.

December 1st

Not much to report, I guess. I do everything on my own these days. I go to the studio alone. I eat alone, and I ride around alone. The tabloids reported that I cracked and entered a mental rehab facility, yet others have me shacked up with Lena in our love nest.

I look like I should be in an episode of Duck Dynasty. I haven't shaved in a month...eh...nobody recognizes me so I'm good with that. Every night, I sit. Alone. Ok well, I'm embellishing a bit. I'm not alone all the time. I've gotten to know a few of the elderly people who live on that side of the block. I liked them even more because to them I was just some lonely kid who hung out on a street bench. They don't know I'm Nate Harper.

Edna lives two buildings down from my bench. She's what they refer to as a 'snow bird'. Normally, she'd be in Florida right now but her husband is stuck at the veteran's retirement rehab because they can't afford a round the clock nurse. I saw her struggling to get her trash out one night about three weeks ago. I've helped her, and the woman in the apartment next to her, out a few times with the trash since then. They've come out and chatted me up quite a bit on the milder nights. Edna told me about her husband two nights ago when she asked if I would mind coming inside to shut off a water valve that was leaking in her bathroom. She didn't have the strength.

When I walked into her place, the first thing I noticed was all the pictures on the wall. I could feel it stirring in the void, creeping its way through my bones. It was like the pizza place deja' vu...one mind fuck coming up. DING. So many pictures of them together, her husband in uniform, the American flag...a purple fucking heart, and he was shoved into some second rate home care facility because they didn't have enough money? This was his home. I quickly took a mental note of his name because by that time I was struggling to keep my shit together. I knew I could've become unhinged after I shut off the valve, so I needed to get the hell out of there. When I walked back out of the bathroom, it was as if I was standing in a different living room. Pictures on a wall...a huge one in the back of the room but I can't make out the faces...an American flag. It's spinning. I turn, and Edna asks if I'm ok...the words...'It was a long time ago' is all I hear instead. In that voice...in her voice.

I let out a huge gust of air when I finished that entry because I didn't even realize I had been holding my breath.

"Oh Nathan, I'm so sorry you had to go through all that."

I played with his hair and watched him sleep for a few minutes before I went to start packing him up for Vancouver, and then check my email and stuff. Nathan's phone kept going off in the kitchen so I went to silence it. I picked it up and saw the text on the screen. It was from Lena.

All set for Vancouver? I'll be on the one o'clock out.

You'll be on what? My stomach got that nervous sick feeling. Why didn't he tell me Lena was going to

VC?

I opened up the text and there was one from last night. It really set me off.

> *You look hot in that suit. You know what would look better on you though? Me.*

About ten minutes later Nathan replied.

> *Stop it Lena*

Next was a pic of her wearing Nathan's suit jacket, with her covering her nose with the fabric like she was smelling it.

Holy shit, I'm going to lose it.

> *Come get your jacket*

> *If it didn't have my keys in it, I'd tell you to keep it.*

> *You'll have to find them first*

> *That's ok. Keep it. I'll get the locks changed*

"It'll be over your chair." I muttered.

All right Jordan. You can go in there and start going off like a crazy lady, or you can ask questions and find out what the fuck is actually going on. One crazy lady comin' up.

I had nothing to say to Lena that wouldn't come across as incriminating in court so I decided to take it to my husband.

"What the fuck is *this shit*, Nathan?" I stomped in our room and threw the phone at his still sleeping head.

Maybe that was a bad idea...no more head trauma.

"Ow! What the fuck, Jordan? What did you do that for? Are you serious right now?" He came back at me.

"Whatever. What is this shit about Lena going to VC and how she'd look hotter on you than your suit?"

My voice got louder and louder with every word.

"Jesus Christ, Jordie." Nathan rubbed his face and got out of bed.

"I told her to knock it off. She was lurking around The London last night. I tried to avoid her, but she kept popping up around corners then disappearing. Then she texted me. I didn't want to upset you with it because I knew the whole Bristol pissing contest must have been emotionally draining enough for you," he said in an annoyed tone.

"Was that fucking sarcasm? A *pissing contest*, Nathan? Really? She's chasing my husband around and it's a pissing contest on my part?"

"Jordan...I thought you understood that there are women...lots and lots of them...even some men...that want what you have. *Me.* What does it matter when all I want is you?" He stood up and shouted at me.

Yeah, his frustration level had capped out. He was going to lose his cool. We rarely fought, and even when we did, it would last five minutes and then all was forgiven. But this shit, hell no...this was serious business and I wanted it handled.

"Why didn't you tell me she was going then? Huh?" I stood solid with my hands on my hips waiting for an answer.

He rubbed his face again and sat on the edge of the bed.

"I didn't know until she caught me at the party last night. She was out in the main restaurant with Eidenberg and Stevens. She's in the running to replace Scarlett because she got pregnant and can't shoot now," he explained.

"And you failed to tell me all this, why again?" I asked in a calmer voice.

"Because I didn't want to upset you for no reason. I planned to let Eidenberg know if she is right for the part, I would have to withdraw from my role. I was going to tell him it wasn't personal. It was more of a creative style difference. Which of course would be a lie but "I hate the bitch" doesn't really work in the big bad world of responsibility."

"Saving me once again, I see...stop. I'd much rather just know what's going on. This way when the headlines read that we're the second generation Jennifer Aniston Brad Pitt, I'm prepared and I'm not blindsided," I snapped back at him.

"Oh my fucking god, you frustrate me." He pulled at his hair with both hands.

"I'm done. I need some air. There's your bag. I'll see ya' when you get home."

I stomped out of the bedroom, down the hall, grabbed my scarf, jacket, gloves, and boots from the entrance closet and headed down to the street. It was starting to snow.

Fucking global warming, and shit. Seventy-one and Margarita's on Tuesday, twenty-nine and blizzard like conditions on Saturday. Makeup your mind, bitch.

I walked the West Side for a few hours. I tried calling Rachel a couple of times but her phone was off. I decided to stop at my favorite Mexican place, Blockhead's, so I grabbed a cab and hit the one over in Midtown East.

I was kinda' glad Rachel didn't answer. She just got engaged and I don't want to be all Debbie Downer on her happy time. I called my sister and talked to her, while I ate. She was always my voice of reason. She never told me how to live my life but she always knew what to say when things weren't going so great, or I was acting like an jackhole.

"Jordan, he was trying to *not* get you all worked up. You're the asshole for even going the 'Jenn and Brad' route. Neither Lena nor Bristol are any Angelina, that's fo sho," Kelly teased me.

I couldn't help but laugh.

"Maybe I overreacted a bit. Nathan did mention quitting the on-screen side of the business. He wants to try some new things. Maybe that was his way of letting me know something wasn't right," I admitted to her.

"You? Overreact? That's doubtful, Jords." She was such a sarcastic twat sometimes.

"Fuck off." I laughed.

"Hey, Kelly, my phone's dying. Nathan's been blowin' it up for the last two hours. Call him and let him know I'm ok that my phone's going to die soon. I wanna save some battery in case of an emergency. Love ya. Doubt it. Byeee," I said before moving to cut off the call.

"Love you more! Doubt it, bye," she said at the same time as me, so I hit End.

As I was digging for my wallet, a text from Evelyn came through.

> *I need to talk to you ASAP. Where are you?*
>
> *Blockhead's Midtown East. What's wrong?*
> *Are you okay? Your daughter? Nathan okay?*
>
> *We're fine. Thanks. Can you meet me at the 59th and East Drive Central Park entrance?*
>
> *Sure give me 30*
>
> *K*

This day was getting more and more frustrating by the minute. I paid and left.

CHAPTER 20

I hopped in a cab and headed back to my new part
of the city. I got out at the Ritz so I could grab a cup
of coffee at the diner before meeting Ev. After the
coffee stop, I made my way to the entrance of the
park, where she was waiting for me.

The snow was letting up a bit so I could see a bit
better, too. She had on a puffy white furry vest
complete with matching hat, a black turtleneck
underneath, all brought together by a gorgeous pink
chevron pattern scarf. The woman could make the
abominable snowman look like a fucking fashionista.
Not that any of this was relevant except for the fact
that I loved her style.

"Look at you, you little snow bunny," I shouted
when she was near enough to hear me.

She turned, but before she could even say hello, a
bunch of shit happened at once.

I heard a horn honk and Evelyn looked back over
her shoulder. I screamed as I watched an SUV hop the
curb, and plow into Evelyn. Her body flew back about

twenty feet and slammed into a concrete wall. The vehicle backed up and dinged into a bicycle rack pole. I assumed it was going to stop but instead it sped off dodging oncoming traffic.

"Evelyn!"

I dropped my coffee and screamed. "Oh my god, someone call 9-1-1. Now!"

I ran to her, fell to my knees and tried to figure out what to do. Blood covered her vest and hat.

Jesus Christ thinnnk Jordan!

I was panicking. I looked around me to see if anyone looked like he or she knew what to do. I started to cry feeling helpless. There were a few people on the phone with 9-1-1 and some asshole was videoing it.

"Put the god damn phone down and help her," I screamed but he ignored me.

I heard a horse galloping up behind me. I sat up straight and saw two police officers on horses. They were so much faster than cars being they could avoid traffic and go up the wrong way on a one-way street.

I took off my coat and put it under her head.

Evelyn started to stir a little, and I breathed a huge sigh of relief.

"It's okay. You're okay, Ev, I'm here with you," I said as calmly as I could muster as I leaned in so she could hear me over all the background clatter.

She moaned a bit and raised her hand slightly.

"No, don't move. Lay still. I'm with ya', mija, right here."

I straightened in time to see the police officers jump off their horses. I took her hand. Thank god, I'd backed away a bit because she suddenly coughed and blood spattered everywhere.

Holy shit. She's going to die.

"You're okay Ev. The police are here with a big ass first aid kit to fix you up. C'mon hang in there with me." I bawled out of control.

"Get back," one of the officers yelled as he moved me out of the way.

An ambulance was turning onto the street and his siren was blaring. I remember being so grateful there was a firehouse and medic on every effin' block of New York City. I couldn't stop shaking, and I just wanted my husband. The man that was making a video pointed his phone at me, and I flipped.

"Are you fucking *kidding me?* There is a woman lying here bleeding out from her head, mouth, who knows where else, and all you do is stand there and record it? It's people like *you* that should be hit by trucks, not good people like her, you piece of shit."

My temper flared. I whacked the phone right out of his hands and I started swinging. Not Mike Tyson swinging, more like Ralphie from a Christmas Story swinging. Flailing out of control, cursing, and crying as I just swung at this guy. Yepp…I cracked. One of the policemen hurried over and pulled me off the guy hauling me back.

"If you can't control yourself, I'm going to have to cuff you and…"

"And what? You gunna' throw me on the back of your horse and toss me in the pokey?" I spat out not thinking.

And yupp…that's exactly what he did.

He handcuffed me and stood with me next to his horse until a squad car could pick me up. Luckily, the jerkoff I took a few swings at didn't want to press any charges. Most men would never stand up in court and confess a woman beat him up. So, his ego saved my ass this time.

I watched as the EMT cut Evelyn's sleeves up the

middle and started an IV. They had her secured on a backboard and put a quick dressing on her head wound. Finally, they lifted her up on the gurney. I saw the paramedic come over, stick a silver thing in her mouth, and began feeding a tube down it as they walked to the ambulance. He asked them to stop for a moment, and placed a bag on her stomach before pulling out the silver thing. Quickly and efficiently, he attached a bag to the end of the tube sticking out of her mouth and it began to fill with liquid. *Blood.*

I stood frozen in horror as they loaded her into the ambulance and closed the doors. Everything rushed through my head at once. *I should be with her. Her family needs to know. I need to get a hold of Nathan so he can look up the numbers in her file. Jesus Ev, please don't die.*

I began sobbing again, and started to shiver.

"Would you like a blanket, Mrs. Harper?" The officer who had me all shackled up asked.

"No, I'm okay. Thanks. Besides I've heard it's cold in cell block D, I'm prepping for my stay." I joked lamely.

"Nah, you're not going to jail, just a holding cell for a bit." He winked and grinned. "Please, can you take these off? I really want to go call her family and wait at the hospital."

"When the guy whose ass you were handing him leaves, I'll spring ya'."

Hallelujah.

I heard my name called out from a distance. I could see two heads bobbing through the now dissipating crowd. Once the circle of rubberneckers spread out a bit, I could see it was Nathan and Frank.

I blew my hair out of my face. *Lovely, just what I need. Nathan, and Frank, seeing me in handcuffs.*

"Jordan. Baby. Are you okay? Jesus fucking Christ,

I just died ten thousand deaths on the way here," he said in a panic as he ran his hands all over my face, my hair, and then threw me into his chest with a bear hug. I couldn't do anything but stand there like a stick of celery because I was still a felon apparently.

"Officer, is she under arrest?" Frank asked.

"No, sir," the officer answered as he put a phone in a plastic bag and sealed it.

"Then what's with the cuffs?" Nathan snapped.

"She was swinging at a bystander. I had to restrain her somehow." As he spoke he shook the bag, and grinned.

"Is that his phone?" I asked.

"Sure is. This has the entire hit and run recorded on it, right down to where you knocked it out of his hands."

"Remove the cuffs, please?" Frank asked.

"As long as Layla Ali over here keeps her hands to herself," The officer said and spun me around.

"Easy," Nathan demanded.

"Easy? Okay, pal. You should be tellin' her that." He undid the cuffs and I immediately started rubbing my wrists.

"I'm so sorry, Nathan." I threw my arms around him and sobbed.

"Well, that's all I need. I have your statement, Mrs. Harper. The precinct will call if they need anything else from you." My personal cop handed me a piece of paper with the incident report number on it in case I needed it.

"My daughter is a huge fan, Mr. Harper," The other officer said as he stuck out his hand to Nathan.

"Ah, tell her thank you, and I appreciate it." Nathan shook his hand and nodded. He really did appreciate his fans just not the insane ones like Delena.

"Let's go get her info, and call her mom and daughter," I said.

"Frank called them on the way over here."

"Wait, how did you even know what happened?" I asked confused.

"Rachel called. Said you were involved in something at the park and it was on the 'Breaking News' of HLN, E¡ and TMZ. She was at the bar finishing last night's stuff when she heard you yelling from the TV. We came right here once we saw the Central Park sign. She and Tyler are on their way to the hospital."

"Who *does that?* Who puts someone on TV that was just involved in a serious accident?" I was disgusted.

"Well, there's a reason you were picked out, I think. Come on. I'll explain on the way to the hospital." Nathan took off his jacket and threw it around me while Frank went out to the street to hail a cab.

"So after you left, Bristol texted and said she had to talk to me. I ignored her because all I could really think about was you. I was worried sick…"

"He was," Frank agreed nonchalantly while looking out the window.

"But then this text came through." He handed me his phone.

I wanted to punch him right in the throat but I couldn't because the picture staring back at me from the phone sucker punched me in the gut.

"You…you did sleep with Lena?" I asked quietly as I fought back the stinging in my nose that would start me crying again.

Frank let out a manly snort and laughed. Nathan turned white as a ghost.

"What? No. What the fuck? No," he said really fast and shook his head.

"Someone posted it on Nate-Nation. Me sleep with

her? Really? Why would I make up shit in my own journal? What, was I trying to fool myself?" Nathan questioned defensively. "If I had slept with her…it'd been in there."

"Is this one of Deloony's pics then?" It clicked suddenly.

"We don't know. My PR team was on this really fast, before *I* even knew about it. Stan called, no shit, literally the moment after the pic was sent to me. It was posted under Delena's account but when the IT guy over at WM went over it with Nate-Nation's IT, they discovered that it was posted from an IP never used before and at a completely different location. A place that has free wifi. They're trying to locate the address. We can't get names without a court order though. Also, there was a key logger phished from the original account and then fifteen minutes after Delena's account posted the pic, a request came through to lock the account due to a stolen password/unauthorized login."

"So nobody could get on and delete it. Brilliant. Sick and twisted, but brilliant," I said.

"Frank, can you get a court order for that stuff?" I asked the best man to know.

"Nope, internet porn holds no bearing on getting taken down. You're dumb enough to take any pic naked then you deserve to be exploited on the Internet," he answered in a 'matter-of-fact' tone. "Just ask my daughter. Which reminds me, she won't be moving here." He threw in quick with a mutter still looking away out the window.

Ummm okay, we can revisit that at a later date…

"It's useless anyway, Jordan. The account will be deleted but so many people have that pic by now that…" Frank stated the obvious.

"Well it doesn't matter, right? It didn't really

happen. There's a pic of you smacking me around and going for Emma next, but that isn't real either. We lived through that. I've seen pics of you really *in bed* with Lena," I said, and Nathan looked at me funny.

"Stills from the movie," I added. He understood then.

"But this is different. This is defamation of character, no? I mean, whoever made that picture is trying to wreck my marriage and who knows, maybe even my career," Nathan inquired.

"Don't pull a muscle," I said patting his knee.

"Pull a muscle? Doing what?" Nathan looked lost.

"Reaching that far with those motives." I stifled my humor but Frank just roared with laughter.

"Oh kid, you're good." He laughed and fist bumped me.

That was what made me laugh.

We pulled up in front of the hospital and Nathan paid the fare before we all got out. Nathan's phone rang. It was Tyler looking for us. Once we got up to the CCU waiting room, we saw Evelyn's mother. She filled us in on her daughter's injuries and condition. The six broken ribs, and a punctured lung were worrisome but the most severe was her lacerated kidney. The rest, they said, she would recover from just fine. They had her in a medically induced coma for the time being to assure no more brain swelling from the concussion. Her mother and daughter had already given their blood to be tested as donors if her kidney doesn't heal on its own within the month. I offered to test as well.

Rachel stood off to the side but made no attempt to volunteer. I side eyed her and she gave me one of her 'what-bitch' faces. I gave my head a little side nod for her to come over to where I was but she ignored me.

"Rachel. You have two kidneys," I said to her and

Nathan looked up at me.

"And they are very happy together. Thank you very much." She sat down. I guess she could feel everyone's eyes on her because she suddenly stood up in a huff.

"Fine, Jesus Christ, I'll test." She snatched the pen and clipboard from the nurse's hand, and started filling it out.

"You know the odds of you being a match are like one in fifty million, so be nice, it's not likely you're actually likely to be one," I said to her trying not to move my lips.

"Okay loud mouth, everyone can hear you anyway. You whisper like an elephant walks," Rachel called me out.

I rolled my eyes and finished filling out the sheet.

After we got our blood taken, I asked the nurse if I could see Evelyn. I knew she was out of it until at least tomorrow but the last images I had of her sucked big time, and I just wanted to get a glimpse of her recovering.

The charge nurse took me up to the CCU where she had round the clock monitoring, and took me to stand outside her room. Evelyn was in a glass box.

"She looks better already," I said to the nurse.

"Yeah, I was in the ER when she came in. I was getting all her info for her room up here while they worked on her. It didn't look good there for a few minutes," She said.

I looked up because a flash caught my eye.

"You guys put the TV on for coma patients?" That clearly stumped me.

"Sure we do. They can hear everything. They aren't unconscious; just in a deep, deep sleep. It's like brain rest," she explained and then nudged me. "Is that you?

Oh, my god, is that Ms. Martinez's accident? What are you doing? Oh...oh, yeah you just let him have it," she described in a hushed whisper what we saw on the TV blow for blow.

"Ugh." I turned away.

"All right. Well, thank you for letting me visit. If anything changes, would you call me? Please. I know HIPAA and all, but I don't need specifics, just general updates. I know Nathan is worried as well...she's his assistant." That's right. I shamelessly used my hot husband to woo the woman.

"I'm sure he is." She touched my hand and smiled.

Oh...looks like I didn't have to use Nathan after all. It looks like I'm more her type.

I don't care who you are when someone hits on you, whether it be the same sex or not, you feel special, and she was cute.

"Thanks so much." I wrote my number down on the paper she gave me.

"Oh, can you take this with you and give it to her mother? Can't have any flowers or gifts in the room so..." She handed me a 'Build-a-Bear' bear that someone had sent for Evelyn.

"Will do." I smiled and headed back down to the café where everyone was waiting for me.

As I approached the door, I heard my name shouted from behind me. Oh, how I wish I hadn't turned around.

UGH! I don't want to deal with you right now.

"Bristol," I said with exaggerated listlessness.

Where there's Bristol, there's Michael. Where is the big oaf anyhow?

"How is she?" Bristol busted out in a dramatic panic.

"If her mother wants to tell you, she can." I pointed the way inside the café.

"Oh how nice, you got her a Bear?" She gave me a small smile.

"Oh, this? No. Someone sent it to Evelyn, but no gifts are allowed in the CCU rooms," I explained while Bristol just stood there…still…making no effort to walk away.

"That's odd. All she has is her mother and daughter. The rest of her family is in Columbia." She snatched the bear from my hands and opened the card.

Ooookay thennn, rude. Open other people's shit.

"Well, that was nice of Lena. Don't you think?" She turned the card to me.

I made zero attempt to look like I gave a flying fuck, or a rolling doughnut, until the name caught my attention.

"Wait. Did you say Lena sent her this?" I asked horridly as I yanked the card from her hand.

"Ow, paper cut, bitch," she yelped.

"Yeah, whatever. You'll live prissy pants. Focus. Lena sent this? How do you know it's from Lena?" I shoved the card in her face and I'll admit it I sounded a bit unstable. Okay, like a fucking lunatic.

"Um, because Lena's real name is Delena Rose. Everyone just calls her Lena."

Shut the front door. Deloony is Delena…Delena is Deloony. Holy shit.

"I am going to kick that mother ffffffff…" I started to say and stopped because Bristol's head began to drip blood down her forehead from her scalp, I guessed.

"Uh. You're bleeding. You okay?" I asked with a disgusted look on my face.

Bristol dabbed the top of her head and when she felt the wetness, I guessed it freaked her out because she got all twitchy and skitzy. Maybe even a bit panicked.

"Dammit. Let me go take care of this. I stood up in

my kitchen and forgot I had a cabinet door open. I bumped right into the corner of it."

"Brutal." I blew her off and went into the café' to inform Nathan of the new development.

CHAPTER 21

We left the hospital around seven that evening. As soon as we walked into the apartment, I headed straight to the bathroom. I pushed my pre-heat shower button, stripped off my clothes and put them in a plastic bag. I headed straight to the kitchen to throw the bag in the trash. When I paraded past Nathan on the way back, he cut his phone call short and followed me to our room.

"I just confirmed it. That *was* Lena's account but she didn't post that last manipulation." He stuck his hand in the shower and pressed number three.

"And you know this how?" I questioned him as I brushed my teeth.

"Because I just hung up with her," Nathan said, and by the look on his face, he was waiting for my reaction.

"Well, that's a plus. One mystery solved. Delena is Deloony but good news, there's someone crazier than her out there who wants a piece of us. *Awesome*," I said in one big fluid sentence with my toothbrush hanging out of my mouth and ended with a two thumbs up accompanied by a cheesy smile. Oh yeah, I did say I was still naked too, right?

I spit and rinsed then stepped in the shower. Nathan followed me. We stood there for a few minutes letting the hot water run over our tense tired bodies.

Today was a doozy for us, both emotionally, and physically. I couldn't wait to get in bed, FaceTime with my mother-in-law because she was driving Nathan up a goddamn wall since she saw me on the news. Also, I wanted to see Nate. I already called Emma and let my sister know I made it home and that I was fine.

Nathan ended up pulling out of his trip to Vancouver, which made me feel better.

So once I accomplished all that needed to be done, and after getting some stress relieving lovin' from Nathan in the shower, I settled into bed.

"Are we having a naked night?" Nathan asked excitedly when he came back from calling Frank and letting the concierge know that we were not to be disturbed by anyone that was not on the approved list.

He stripped and hopped into bed. I immediately clung to him. He didn't even have a chance to get comfortable. I wrapped my arms, legs,, and my entire body around him. I just let everything go. I knew he would never cheat on me. Our fight wasn't necessary but it's good to disagree or just bitch each other out every now and again. It keeps shit interesting and ventilated. Oh, and the making up part was the best part of it because it could get so intense. In that 'I-can't-move-my-limbs-after-that' sort of way that stayed with you into the next day.

"Babe," I said.

"Yeah."

"I'm sorry I over reacted," I apologized.

"Don't be. Truth be told, I'd react the same exact way if it was a picture of you." He kissed my forehead.

"So, what did Lena have to say? Is she going to publicly apologize then close her account?" I asked.

"The fucking Head Master to the School of Crack-Pots." I muttered under my breath.

"Yes and no. She said she would put up a public apology for the things she'd said in the past. The disrespectful picture and disparaging comments towards you and let everyone know she met up with us and resolved things. And Nordie is 'for sure legit'." He paused. "Hashtag YOLO Hashtag LoveNotHate Hashtag Hashtag," he added.

I busted out laughing with what little energy I had left.

"Don't do that ever again," I teased.

"Hashtag LoveMyWife," he slipped in as I laughed.

"So, what's next? How do we find out who really posted the pic?" I wondered out loud.

"We wait for Frank to gather all the security footage from the location it was sent from that day and go from there." He shrugged.

We both must have fallen asleep because Nathan and I were both out of it when we woke to the doorbell ringing over, and over.

"What now?" Nathan complained as we both rolled out of the bed still half-asleep.

We both threw on some clothes and shuffled out of the bedroom to see who was at the door.

I glanced at the clock.

"It's only nine thirty?" I yawned. The doorbell rang again, and then one more time.

"All riiight already, damn," I yelled as I approached

the door.

"Who is it?" I pressed the speaker.

"It's Leon from concierge, Mrs. Harper. I'm so sorry to bother you. I know Mr. Harper said you weren't to be disturbed for any reason, but this is an emergency," he spoke through the door.

"What's going on, now?" I complained as I opened it.

"My apologies again, ma'am, there is a *gentleman* downstairs who is in need of medical assistance but refuses to leave unless he speaks with one of you. I told him I would call the police and he encouraged me to do so, and then passed out on the floor. The police and Paramedics are on the way, but I thought I should inform you. Do you know this man?" Leon asked as he handed me a license.

"Oh my god, yes! Where is he?" I screamed and Nathan was next to me in a second.

"Where is he?" Nathan snapped.

"In the lobby," Leon answered with a jump.

I don't think he expected us to know who the man was.

"Oh, oh no. Okay. Well. Let's get back down there then." Poor Leon suddenly looked frantic.

We hurried into the hallway. As a threesome, we stared at the slow as molasses elevator that would take ten years to get to us and back to the lobby.

"The stairs," I shouted to Nathan but Leon seemed to think that was a bad idea.

"Those have an alarm," he yelled out but I was already through the door when the sirens began to blare.

Undetered, we zipped down ten floors and busted through the emergency door when we saw the 'G' above it. Nathan was right behind me when I got to Mike. A paramedic had already begun working on him. Mike had an oxygen mask on and his head was full of gashes and bruises.

"Mike. What happened?" I cried as Nathan and I knelt next to him on the floor.

"He's unconscious," the medic yelled. "You have to move!"

The EMT pushed me out of the way.

Just as they got him on the gurney, Bristol came running in.

"Here he is, thank god. I've been calling him and calling him," she said out of breath.

"Which hospital are you taking him to?" I shouted to the EMT.

"Lenox Hill," The EMT answered me as they left through the doors.

"I've had enough of hospitals and people being all fucked up for a lifetime," I screamed as I hit the elevator button.

"Can I hitch a ride with you guys? I can't drive in the city. It gives me panic attacks," Bristol asked meekly.

So the life sucking bitch has a weak side. I never would have guessed.

When we got upstairs, I told Bristol to have a seat and we'd be out in a few minutes. I really was in no mood to play the hostess with the mostess. I'd had a hellish day and the night wasn't lookin' too hot either.

"Jordie, could you throw this out for me please?" She moved to hand me a crumpled up tissue or something.

Bitch, I am not your boogie rag thrower outer.

"I got it." Nathan took it from her without hesitation and threw it out.

"Thanks," she said less than enthusiastic.

As we walked down the hall, he smelled his hand.

"It smells like mint oil or something. It's oily," he complained.

"Probably some of her voodoo juice. The evil bitch is trying to kill me," I said with a laugh as we walked into our room.

Nathan went straight to the bathroom to wash his hands.

"Babe, I'll meet you out in the living room. I don't need her trying to steal anything else," I complained as I grabbed my sneakers and sweater.

When I came back out from the bedroom, all dressed and ready to go for hospital trip number two, Bristol was looking at a photo album…that I'd had nowhere in plain sight.

Make yourself at home and rummage through my personal shit…by all means.

"You were so young in these," Bristol commmented as she turned the page.

"Yep. I'd just moved back to the big apple," I said grabbing a water out of the fridge.

"Want one?" I offered her a bottle.

"I'm okay, thanks."

"So, what happened with Mike? You said you were trying to get a hold of him?" I asked her as I leaned up against the wall.

"Yeah, well, he dropped me off around three o'clock at Bergdorfs and I walked up Fifth Ave a bit to get some fresh air. You know. Enjoying the snow," she said flipping a page.

"Oh, did you hear all the commotion then by the park while you were at BD?"

"No, I was inside so I didn't hear a thing."

The way she dismissed what I had said was eerie. It was like a rehearsed answer.

"When I saw it was snowing, I decided to take a

walk. It never snows in California," she reiterated with a sigh as she turned another page.

"Well in Tahoe it does, but not in SoCal."

I gave a nervous laugh and checked my phone for the time.

"Tick Tock Nathan. Let's go," I yelled.

"So what, did you take a cab home?" I asked trying to make small talk while waiting for Nathan.

Seriously honey...you're worse than me sometimes.

"No, I didn't go home. I walked around and then I called Mike."

"But I thought you said you hit your head on a cabinet at home before you got to the hospital?" I looked at her like she had two heads.

"Nathan, *Come on,*" I yelled down the hallway, again.

Bristol was still looking at my old as hell photo album that had every picture of Jason chopped out. Talk about uncomfortable.

"Hey, are you okay? You're sugar isn't dropping or anything is it? Because normally you go from zero to bitchy in no time, but right about now you're just in a fucking 'creeping me out zone'," I said as walked over to her.

Wait, that isn't even my photo album. What the fuck is happening?

"It never snows where I live," Bristol repeated.

"Yeah, got that. No snow. SoCal. Did you get that bump checked out on your head? You seem to be off."

By a lot, you crazy bitch.

"Never snows in Santa Anna." She looked up at me. Her face was blank.

"Um, yeah, okay. NATHAN," I screamed this time.

I was about to use our family code word but I sized her up. I could probably take her if she went off so I waited.

Bristol stood up holding a picture in her hand.

"How come you haven't anything of your first husband's around?" Bristol asked as she examined the room.

"FLAP JACK, Nathan FLAP FUCKING JACK," I screamed.

"He can't hear you. He's...napping." Bristol giggled like a fucking psychopath.

"What did you do to my husband, you bitch?" I stepped forward but she had a Taser gun.

"Oh jesus...another fucking nut case? Really God? Really?" I asked looking up at the ceiling. "What, we didn't meet your status quo of the lifetime head count of fucking people that are out of their minds?" I continued.

"Shut up, Jordie. So cool. You have all the answers, you and that stupid bitch best friend of yours. You two just have fun little comebacks for everything, don't you? Pretty little bitches. Especially you. The pretty little bitch that steals people's boyfriends and then laugh about it while the other person cries."

This bitch has crazy Jody Arias eyes.

"It never snows for Bristol in Santa Anna," she said quietly with wide eyes.

What is this fucking nut doing? Is this a riddle?

"Bristol, I have no idea what's going on with you, but..."

Oh. Shit. It never snows for Bri Stole in Santa Anna. Bristol Santana. Holy fucking laser beams this is Brianna Stoltsen. Jason's ex.

Flap Jack! Flap Jack!

This shit right here was what the I.D. Channel made mini- series out of—my life.

"You bitch. After you took him from me once, you just couldn't leave us alone. You had to steal him away, didn't you?" Bristol screamed at me.

"God dammit, when will you stop fucking up my life, Jason?" I started screaming and stomping my foot.

"I didn't want him the second time. You could have kept that shit. To be honest, I didn't want him the first time, but the motherfucker knocked me up because he knew I'd make it work. He knew how much I wanted a baby. And how the hell do you look so young still, and manage to break into the Hollywood scene at your age?" I said all at once.

"He came back to me. He was going to get Emma and we were going to move back overseas. We had it all planned. Then you just fucked it all up." Bristol began pacing.

Fuck.

"What do you want from me Brist…Bri?" I tried to reason with her.

"Nathan. It's only fair. You took away the love of my life…twice. Seems reasonable, doesn't it?"

"Jordie?" I heard Nathan call me.

"Nathan."

"So Nathan's up. Good. Let's go pay him a visit," Bristol said with a blank stare and a fake cheery smile.

"No." I stood in front of her.

"Go. Or I fry your ass and leave it to rot at an abandon port on Roosevelt island like I did ol' Mikey boy. See how well that worked though. I need to work on the dosage of that stuff. He was just supposed to drown quietly when the tide came in, but he woke up before that happened. Of course, I could just run your fat ass over like I did Evie. That bitch was soft. She lacked a backbone. She was about to tell you everything," Bristol ranted and shoved me forward.

"Move," she demanded.

When she shoved me through the doorway of my room, I saw Nathan on the floor. I knelt down there with him and asked him how he was feeling.

Bristol just stood there staring at us when Frank, like a fucking Ninja, popped out from the bathroom and tackled her to the floor. Once he'd cuffed her, he stood her upright.

"Ah yes, Frank. Jason counted on you being here to save the day, so predictable. I bet Jason that you'd never catch on quick enough, but he was right yet again," She giggled like the crazy person she was. "Why don't you take a peek and see what's under my shirt on my back."

Frank spun her around and lifted up her shirt. The bitch had a bomb strapped to her.

She stuck her tongue out at him and exposed a small capsule looking thing in her mouth.

"Once I bite down on this…boom goes the dynamite. Jason, I love you."

Bristol took a deep breath, and we all screamed *no* together before she bit down. We all stood there too scared to move.

"Jordan, am I dead this time?" Nathan asked.

"Well, if you are, at least you remember me this time," I answered.

"Not funny. What happened?" Nathan looked at Frank with a confused expression. We all stared at Bristol as she chomped down on that detonator between curses.

"What Jason didn't count on was you being a dumbass and hiring Mike to spite Jordan. Mike saw the bomb in your bag this morning. He also knew you tried to kill Evelyn so that's why you tried to get rid of him. Let's talk about what you didn't know. You didn't know that the bottle of chloroform you've got there, mixed with tea tree oil and mint to mask the smell, isn't chloroform at all. It's alcohol mixed with tea tree oil and mint. Mike took care of that when you were at the hospital talking to Jordie, while setting up Lena for the leaked picture," Frank explained while Nathan and I sat on the floor dumbfounded just staring at him.

"And now you're supposed to say 'I would have gotten away with it, if it wasn't for those meddling kids," I exclaimed looking at Bri dead serious, and then busted out laughing.

"What? You told me I was cool and always had a comeback for everything. I couldn't let you down now, could I, Bri?"

I stood up as Frank made a call.

"Come on up, I've got her," he said and hit End.

"Oh, oh, tell her what she's won now, Frank." I was relentless, I'd had the second shittiest day of my life and I was going to make something good of it somehow.

"Well Jordan," Frank said as grabbed Bri by the cuffs and led her down the hallway. Nathan and I followed behind. "She's won a trip to a maximum security federal prison while she waits out the three, maybe four months, until her arraignment where she will be charged with aiding and abetting a terrorist as well as accessory to multiple war crimes, kidnapping, harboring a felon, and a harboring an enemy of the country. Shall I go on?" he asked.

"Naahhh. That's ok." I waved bye to her as they hauled her out.

I looked Nathan over.

"You okay?" I ran my hands all over his head and arms, and examined his face.

"I am," he said. "Is there anyone else in your past I have to worry about?"

He nudged me.

"Fuck if I know anymore at this point. But hey, at least she didn't get very far in the killing us department." I winked at Frank.

"Thanks man." Nathan hugged him.

"No need that's what I'm here for." Frank replied.

"And you thought we wouldn't need you anymore," I commented to Frank teasingly.

"How's Mike?" I asked suddenly, remembering what happened to him.

"He's fine. He had an ischemic attack which made him pass out. He just texted me, they're keeping him overnight for observation."

"Well, he isn't getting his job back," I quipped.

Frank and Nathan both gave me a look.

"Actually, he won't need your job. The sale on the Middletown office didn't go through. He's going to head it up for me until he can get the credentials and money to take it over," Frank said. "He really does need to move on with his life, Jordan. Remember how hard it was for you to see Nathan with the girls in the magazines? That's how he feels. He needs to let you go and he can't do that while he's under your thumb," Frank lectured me.

"Got it," I answered knowing Frank was right.

"Now can I go to bed since I know he will be okay? Please? I *really* want this day to be over," I begged the powers to be.

Nathan's phone was ringing. "It's my mom. I'll take this in the other room."

He gave Frank a hug and then me a kiss.

"I'll see you in a few," I said as he walked away.

"Frank. Thank you. Thank you for putting Nathan before everything. I don't know what I'd do without you." I reached up and hugged him.

"Well, you better figure it out soon because I'm

going on a five week cruise with Annie next month." He smiled.

"Holy shit, really? Frank. Oh my god, I'm so happy for you," I squealed.

"Well, Nathan and I have been chatting a lot about him taking some time off from on screen and maybe doing some more work behind the scenes. Hence the man cave back there." He nodded towards the studio.

"Yeah, he mentioned something about taking some time off," I said with a smile.

"He'd do anything for you, you know that?" He kissed my forehead.

"I know. I'm pretty effin lucky," I gushed.

"He's pretty effin lucky, too." Frank put his fist up, and I laughed.

"Please don't make it go boom," I teased.

"Ohhhh good one. Ya lucky punk." He laughed and we bumped knuckles.

CHAPTER 22

I'd just gotten back from dropping Evelyn off at home after physical therapy when I saw the letter from the hospital sitting on the counter.

"Babe?" I called out to Nathan and dropped my bags on the kitchen table.

"Nathan?" I called out again when I heard him talking as I walked down the hallway.

"Sure thing, Eidenberg. I look forward to it. Me, too. Very excited. I'll send it over ASAP." He paused when he saw me, leaned close, and gave me a quick kiss.

"She's doing better. Yeah, in fact, Jordan just got back from bringing her to physical therapy." Nathan stood silent as he listened. "Yeah, I'm my own assistant until she's well enough to work. No temps for me. I'm not up for new people in my life right now." He chuckled. "All right, sir. Talk soon."

He put his obnoxious wireless operator looking headset on the table and swooped in on me for a real kiss.

"Is that a roll of quarters in your pocket or are you just happy to see me?" I joked.

"I am always happy to see you."

Nathan took my hand and slipped it in the waistline of his pants.

He looked yummy, too, with faded jeans hanging off him just so, with a hole in the knee and one by the zipper. I think I probably wore that particular hole there because anytime he put those jeans on; I rubbed up against him like a horny cat.

"Fifteen minutes until my mom gets here." He bit my neck and then sucked on the same spot.

"Ahh, can't today. But how 'bout tomorrow?" I reluctantly declined. "Last day for my monthly visitor."

"You know I don't mind. A little mess never killed anyone." He kissed me again.

"Gross." I turned and picked up the donor letter from the hospital.

"Thank god, Ev didn't need a donor, but I wonder if I was a match." I held up the envelope.

"Well open it and look."

I did and read it silently then put it down.

"I'm not a match. In fact, they ran it through the entire database and I'm not a good match for anyone." I sulked. "Nobody wants my kidney."

I stuck my lower lip out in a pout.

"Baby, I'll take your kidney any day." He grabbed my ass and then smacked it.

"That's not my kidney," I teased.

"Are you sure? Come here let me make sure." Nathan pulled me in close again and groped me with both hands.

"Nope, look at that you're right, it's not a kidney after all. But I still want it." He smacked it again.

"Staaahhhp. You know what happens when you start that shit." I wiggled my butt.

The elevator dinged and we separated.

"You're mom's early." I walked to the door and opened it before she could knock.

"Where's my boy?" I asked when I fully opened it but it wasn't Fiona. It was Rachel and she looked rough.

"Hey, what's up?" I pulled her inside.

"Can I hang out for a little bit?" Rachel asked but her shoes were already off and she was halfway down for the count on my couch.

"Rachel, have you been…drinking?" I asked her. I'm sure I sounded confused because I *was* confused.

"Rachel, you stink like a bowery bum."

"Yepp. I've added daytime drunk to my resume. Check." She slurred face down in my couch.

"Okay, why?" I sat down and moved her hair off her face when she turned her head, so she could breathe better.

"Why not?" She threw her one arm up, then dropped it to the floor and laughed.

Oh man. She's really lit.

"Well, I'm going to make some phone calls…" Nathan said backing out slowly.

"No, no, I want you to stay for this and hear me." Rachel announced.

She attempted to hold herself up and speak, but only one of those things was happening, and that was speaking because well, it didn't take as much strength.

"I got a letter today from the Donor Club of America," Rachel slurred and sat up, her head rolling back and forth until she stabilized it, then she blew the curls out of her face.

"Yep, the DCA sent me my membership letter." She

gave me a single thumb up then let her hand drop with a thud on her lap.

"Rachel, what the fuck is the DCA? There's no such thing as the Donor's Club of America." I tried so hard to hide my laugh but she knew me...even drunk she knew me.

"Don't laugh at me, Bitch. Go look at the letter. In my bag. Hey you, hot guy that gives up a million dollar career for this sack of tits here..." At that point, Rachel pulled a Diana Ross-Lil' Kim moment and pretty much felt me up.

"But what nice ones they are." She snorted. "You have impeccable taste by the way...fetch me my bag, please."

Rachel held her arm up as if she was giving a royal command and then it swung down to her lap.

Nathan just shook his head and gave a quick laugh while he handed over her bag.

"Yank thooo. I mean...Thank you," she said.

"I'm calling Tyler to come get her," Nathan mumbled to me.

"You do that. Please do. He won't come and get me. He isn't going to want all these damaged goods." Rachel ran her hand up and down her neck to her head and back down.

"Read the damn letter," she snapped at me.

"Fine." I fished it out of her purse and opened it up.

"Out loud. Like that Twilight kid said, 'Say it. Out loud.'"

She busted out in an uncontrollable laugh and then stopped. "Okay, read it now."

Christ, she's tanked.

"Dear Ms. Fallon,

Blah, blah, blah, we thank you, yadda, yadda, yadda, we regret to inform you that you are not a match for the specific patient you tested for. However, there are many people in need of live donors and with your consent, (see checked box no. 3) we ran your stats in the patient database. We have great news. You are a match for someone in need of a live donor. Please call my office at your earliest convenience to discuss a possible DNA match with said patient.

All the best,

Alice Leevy"

Da fuq?

"Rachel, you have a brother or a sister? That's amazing. Are you going to call and find out?" I handed her back the paper.

"Or a father," she slurred out.

"Oh, I didn't think of that." *Oops.*

"He didn't want me when he was healthy and I was a kid, but I bet you that ugly ass vase over there he'll want me now." Rachel slumped over on her side again on the couch.

"Well, first of all, I'm not betting you something I already own. And if it's so ugly why would you want to bet it? If you win, you win the ugly vase." I tried to get her mind off the problem at hand.

"Don't try your double talk hocus pocus with me, bitch. And I want to win it so I can smash it." She hiccupped and then laughed.

I couldn't help it, I laughed, too.

Nathan came back out and announced that Tyler was on his way. It seemed she'd been gone since five in the morning or maybe longer. Five was when Tyler got up and realized she was gone.

"Four," Rachel shouted and then I think she passed out.

Nathan just stared at me with a look of uncertainty.

"What?" I asked.

"Four am or is she dreaming of teeing off at the ninth hole?" He gave a quick laugh.

"Look at her. Who the hell knows?" I shook my head.

Tyler came to collect Rachel and drag her home. He'd been worried sick about her all day. When I asked him why he didn't call me to see if she was here, he told me he'd tried but I didn't answer.

"Ugh, sorry. I get shoddy service out by Ev's PT."

Tyler scooped her up and carried her down to the car service and with Nathan's help, got her in the car. We said goodbye to Tyler.

"Call me later dude. Let me know how she's doing." Nathan and he did that half-assed bro-hug.

Meanwhile, Fiona was getting out of a different car.

"Well, look who's fashionably late,." I teased her. She was dressed to the nines.

"Hot date tonight eh?" I asked. "Spin around, let me see the back of that dress."

Fiona handed the baby to me and then spun around slowly.

"Snazay lady. Ready to pound that concrete jungle. Where ya' headed?"

"We're taking swing lessons over at Copello's." She absolutely beamed.

"Ohh really? Swing lessons you say. Well, have fun and be careful."

I gave her a kiss and Nathan gave her a quick hug, and a big smile. I loved it when he smiled so bright his eyes shined.

"Look at your daddy. Look at him. You are going to be quite the heartbreaker when you grow up kid," I said to Nate, and Nathan leaned over and kissed me.

"All right you two, enough already. Let me kiss my girl goodbye." Fiona leaned over and kissed my forehead.

"And now my favorite boy,." she said and when Nathan leaned over, she bent and kissed the baby.

I tried to hold back a laugh but a little one squeaked by.

"Ma? What the hell?" Nathan complained with a laugh.

"What? You had to know you got demoted back to the kid's table when this one came home," She teased him.

"Goodbye Mom, don't kill dad swingin'," he teased her and she smacked his arm.

"Why do you have to be so mouthy? I'm your mother,." she teased him back. "Now give me a kiss and be a good boy."

"Bye Ma, have fun," I said, took Nate's hand and had him wave goodbye, too. She blew him kisses as the car pulled away.

"So your parents are swingers?" I busted out laughing.

"Yeah, right. Imagine that. My mother would shank a bitch if they went near my father," he joked.

"I think it's amazing how they're still so in love after all these years." I bounced Nate up and down.

The kids were out like lights by eight so Nathan and I shared a long hot relaxing bath and maybe a little bit more than that. By nine fifteen, Nathan was out cold as well.

I sat on the chaise and stared out at the city while I mindlessly rubbed lotion on my legs. I took off my robe and slipped a shirt and panties on.

I wiped my hands of the excess lotion and got in bed. I watched Nathan sleep for a minute until I realized I was doing it and decided it was way fucking creepy. I knew I wouldn't in anyway ever want someone watching me sleep.

I picked up Nathan's journal and opened it. We read past Halloween already so things couldn't be too bad after that. I could read it without him.

December 6th

I am happy to report that Private Dominick Cucuzzo is warm in his own bed just in time for Christmas.

Also, I overheard Mom asking Tyler if he would mind picking up the kid's Christmas presents, and find out what size boots for the mamma, and if Rachel would mind wrapping them up as a favor for her. I'm past confusion...I'm on a mission. Oh, and I shaved the beard. It was time.

RIP Beard.

December 10th

It's 3 am. This is the third night I've woken up in a panic from the same dream. It's her...calling my name over, and over. I have my arms around her but she's trying to get away from me. The blood is from her lip but I can't see her face...I hurt her? Is this what everyone is trying to hide from me? I'm a woman-beating monster. Is this what they don't want me to know? If this is true...I'm a coward and I don't deserve to be protected from the truth.

I looked ahead after the last entry I read to see how much remained. There was only one more entry left so I decided I wanted him to read it with me.

"Babe. Wake up." I nudged him.

He mumbled a bit then wrapped his arm around me. I knew what would wake him up. I took his hand and slid it down my shorts under my panties. The man had a knack for knowing what was in his hand and how to work it. Right away, I could feel him stir and I pressed his hand against me harder. That was all it took. He took his free hand, grabbed under my kneecap, and yanked me down so we were face to face.

"You needed something?" He worked his fingers a little faster with the slightest bit more of pressure.

"Uh huh," I moaned as I kissed him.

"What do you need?" Nathan stopped, rubbed up and down, and then in.

Rinse, repeat, I was a mess.

"I wanted you to read your last entry with me." I grabbed his shoulder and bit down just how he liked it.

"Did you say entry? If you insist, ma'am." He rolled onto his back taking me with him so I was on top.

"Say it again," he said grabbing my hips and sliding me across him.

The material between us was getting wetter and wetter. He knew what he was doing to me and he loved it.

"Entry." I leaned down and kissed him, then laughed.

"Good girl." He slid his hands under my shirt, and took one breast in each hand and tugged.

"Oh god."

I reacted the only way I knew how when he pulled that slow and steady rubbin' and tuggin' shit. I came apart and he immediately had his hand between my legs to feel it. He loved to feel what he did to me, and it was when Nathan lost control.

He lifted me off him, guided my head down, and pulled me up by my hips up and got behind me. He tore my panties off and alternated kisses and smacks while he rubbed one out because he wanted it to last. He came and took no mercy on me as he lined himself up and pushed into me before he was even finished. I felt the last of it inside me.

He wrecks me every time. I swear the man took

multiple orgasm classes...no pun intended. He and I knew what each other wanted, when we wanted it, and how we wanted it and amazingly, it was never a repeat episode. It was always something new each time, yet familiar and safe. I truly believe a higher power created Nathan and me for one another. He's my perfect match.

I could feel it building again as he went deeper and deeper with each thrust. When he touched me, I was done again. He wrapped his hand around the front of me and played me until my entire body twitched, and it was one continuous wave after another.

Then he suddenly stopped and got off the bed.

"Stand up and wrap your legs around me,." Nathan commanded me.

Yessss sir.

"With pleasure."

I slipped around him. He kissed me and sucked on me until we reached the window. He brought us down to the ground with his back to the window me on top.

"Keep your eyes open the whole time understand? Watch the city go by. I want to see everything in your face. Don't hold back." He bit down on my neck and took my breast in his hand as his guided himself in with the other.

I didn't make it thirty seconds before he had me where he wanted me again. I closed my eyes and he grabbed my hips hard and tugged me back and forth.

"Open them. Look at me."

Fuck. That's all it took. I'd come undone again and I could feel it was almost his time so I picked up the pace and the pressure, ten seconds later he was mine all over again.

CHAPTER 23

December 13th

Tonight was the night. I had every intention of getting the truth out of Tyler tonight. It was a weekend so the bar closed late. I knew he'd be there to wait for Rachel. I'd watch him every weekend get there between 10 and 11pm. They'd leave about 3am.

Tonight was the night. I was done allowing them to shelter me from whatever wrong I did. I probably deserved to get shot. I blanked it out for a reason.

I saw the bouncer bring something over to the building. The kid answered.

Jesus Christ, I'd turned into a stalker. Edna came down tonight to bring me some hot chocolate and tell me the good news. Her Dominick was home. Of course, I already knew that.

She told me that a Secret Santa had volunteered to pay for all his medical needs at home with a live-in nurse for as long as he needs it, along with basic housing expenses. She handed me the hot chocolate and gave my other hand a squeeze. When she said,

"God bless whoever opened their heart like this to us." I couldn't help but get all choked up from the tears in her eyes.

She told me she had to get back inside, it was cold, and she and Dominick liked to watch reruns of Murder She Wrote together. Before she went inside, she patted my cheek and said, "You're a good boy, I can see it in your eyes and ya know, Nate, I never noticed that without that beard you could be in the movies...I'd even bet the next James Dean."

I laughed and suddenly I didn't feel like a bad guy...I knew I couldn't have hurt any woman, the voice because...I felt odd...what was this feeling? Happiness? But even more so another emotion took the wheel and nailed the gas pedal. I was doing Mach 5 straight into a feeling that overwhelmed me...it was love. I LOVED someone just like that. Edna was me. Metaphorically of course...but I loved someone like she loved her Dominick. Real, raw and everlasting. I just had to find her. And something real told me she was behind that door across the street.

As I approached the building, I could hear 'It's the most wonderful time of the year' playing from the roof. I stared at the steps for a minute then I took in a deep breath, walked up the stoop, and pressed the buzzer. After about 30 seconds, I went to ring it again when my heart stopped.

I heard a kid's voice ask, "Who is it?" I said I was sorry but then I asked if I knew who lived in the building. I saw the curtain move upstairs. After another few seconds, I heard muffled shouting coming from up there as well. I began to doubt my decision to face this head on. Then I heard it...the voice...her voice...a bit shaky but I'd know that voice anywhere.

Go away was all she said. I asked if I knew her or if I knew someone that lives or maybe lived there before.

That I had an accident a few months back and I don't remember much but I know that this place is like a magnet that draws me in. I told her that she doesn't need to be afraid, I'm not dangerous, or anything like that, but that I just couldn't stay away.

Holy shit, had I sounded desperate and scary?

When she finally replied, she sounded like she was about to cry. All I heard was, "You don't know who lives here, Nathan. Now please go away."

That was it. NATHAN. Nobody called me Nathan except her...well, the voice who I now know is her...The rest of the world calls me Nate.

"Oh." Was my grand response. IDIOT. OH? My god, I was the world's biggest pussy.

I needed to pull my shit together quick. I waited a few more seconds then asked her how she knew my name if I didn't know who lived there. When she spoke this time, it was strong and annoyed. She said that everyone knows who Nate Harper is. She told me she has security cameras and can see me.

She was a crafty one, I'll give her that much but I wasn't letting her slip away that easy. Then I cornered her with everyone does know Nate Harper...but she called me Nathan.

She came back over the speaker and begged me to leave. I stayed there for a few minutes just looking around trying to figure out my next move. When I came up with nothing that wouldn't end with a restraining order against me, I walked away.

I got about three buildings down when I heard someone curse. I jogged back to her stoop. She was facing her door doing some weird yoga bend, or what looked like one, trying to pick up her keys. I teased her about what an interesting trick she was performing and asked if I could help her. She scooped her keys up in a hurry and said she didn't need help. I waited for her to turn around but she didn't. I started towards her, and asked her if she was who I just spoke with, and to please don't be scared. When I got within about three feet of her, I had no control. Auto-pilot took over and I was pretty sure I was going to crash and burn after this one, but I didn't give a fuck. I knew she was everything to me somehow and I didn't even know who she was. I had to keep talking or I was going to lose it. I was behind her by that point and when I got a whiff of her hair, a shower came to mind. I know. Fucking weirdo, right?

I told her that I didn't mean to upset her that I was just at a loss in my life right now and how empty and alone I felt. That I couldn't understand for the life of me why this building comforted me so much.

Hey, it was better than I stalk this building to stay sane, ok? I didn't know what to do because she was quiet again but I could hear her sniffle, and then I saw her shoulders move. She was crying. Holy good Christ…going there was a bad idea. I saw her take in a deep breath and she asked me to, 'just go'. I inched forward so I was nearly touching her. She smelled like home. I knew this was the one. I had to know what I did to make her so upset that she couldn't even look at me. She turned around and looked up at me. I had no words. Her eyes locked with mine. Gorgeous green eyes…eyes that sucked the air out of me. All I could do was tell her how beautiful she was.

What she said next threw me off. She disagreed with me because she wasn't a skinny blonde skank as she stared at her belly. I tried to explain that I was just trying to find myself…she came back at me with something about finding more than just myself. My expression must have affected her because her face turned bright red and she looked like she was going to punch me but then, boom went the dynamite, because she exploded. She laid into me about all the women I had been with over the last 6 months, "all the sex", and even used the words, Sexcapade and Sexual Olympics.

That broke me...I cracked a smile and at first, she did too, but then she was all serious again. When she was finally finished, I said I wasn't quite sure why I was discussing my sex life with her but I felt like I was supposed to, so I told her that I don't remember the last time I'd had sex. Literally. She didn't believe me.

Wow, this firecracker had quite the mouth on her. I loved it. I told her I had nothing in common with them but then Tyler showed up calling my name and dragging me off for a beer next door. I caught some facial expressions and hand gestures between them before we walked off.

When we got inside the bar, it was still packed but they were winding down. Apparently, I wasn't popular with anyone who worked there...especially the big guy over in the corner...he was definitely trying to shrink my head with his mind. No doubt about it. I saw Rachel answer her phone and then glare over at me...she wanted to blow my head up not shrink it.

We sat and waited for them to close up, clean up, and get out of there. It was nearly 3am. Everyone was gone, it was just Tyler, Rachel, and me left in the quiet bar.

Rachel tossed her stuff on the counter in a huff and stood quietly...giving me her all familiar dirty look. This can't be good...she's quiet. I told Rachel I don't know what it is I did exactly...and that's when it happened. She exploded. Hands flailing, screaming curses, she grabbed her phone and started playing some boy band song. She jumped on the bar, and started dancing. I thought she'd truly lost her mind. Then she rambled on about Jordie, Emma, and a baby. How a crazy ass terrorist who was actually Jordie's presumed dead, but who'd actually flipped on our country, husband had attacked me.

I mean words were flying everywhere and they made no sense. I pushed off the bar and headed outside. I needed to breathe. I needed air. Jordie? Jordie...Jordie.

I'd just got to the street when BAM, flash after flash, went off in my mind. It was all back. Every single detail. Every single memory. I held my head where I was hit. I ran over to her building. JORDAN MARIE SPAGNATO. Emma...Emma was the kid...and the baby. Our baby. HOLY FUCKING SHIT. It's all there.

I ran back in the bar and yanked Rachel into my arms. I just started screaming, thank you, holy shit, THANK YOU. I swear I almost broke her...she is so tiny and I was swinging her around like a rag doll. Tyler stopped me, and saved Rachel. He was smiling. They both were. I remembered!

I needed to get over there. I needed to...no wait. I had a better idea.

Rachel...ohhhh! Rachel had wanted to tell me something all along. She laughed and told me that she was just trying to shrink that big ass head of mine. I started laughing. I asked if she could let me in so I could get to the rooftop. I'd wait for Jordie there. Thankfully, she agreed.

Rachel let me up. I saw the wireless speaker things sitting on the table so I synced my phone with it and searched for the song and played it. A few minutes later, I heard the door open. I turned and there she was...messy hair...sleepy-eyed, and angry as hell from the looks of it. She could have had a Saint Bernard on her head and she still would have been the most beautiful woman I had ever laid eyes on.

There she was. My Jordie.

That's really about it. I don't have the time to go through the rest because I just heard Emma wake up. I want to go downstairs and surprise her. I won't wake Jordan.

But, that's how I ended up Finding Nathan.

I closed up his journal and placed it on my nightstand.

"And here we are." I smiled.

"Here we are." He gave a quick laugh.

"You beat my vag up you know, it's off limits for at least two days," I scolded him playfully.

"Oh no. I can kiss it and make it better," he offered.

"Just kiss me." I leaned in.

"Anytime, anyplace, sweetheart." My Nathan obliged sweetly.

His phone was buzzing but he ignored it. After a few minutes, it buzzed again but he still paid it no mind.

When we woke in the morning, it was still going off so he finally checked it.

"Babe, it's Tyler. Have you heard from Rachel?" Nathan asked sitting up and patting me on the leg to wake me thoroughly.

"No, why? Not since we threw her in the drunk tank." I joked stifling a yawn.

When he didn't respond but kept reading the texts, I knew something was up.

"What's wrong?" I panicked and grabbed my phone off my nightstand. There were no new calls or texts.

"I got nothing. You?"

"I just texted asking him where he was because I'd come meet up with him, and help," Nathan answered.

His phone went off again and he read the text. His face was expressionless.

"What does it say? Nathan? Is she okay?" I fired off the questions in rapid-fire succession as my panic increased.

He read the text aloud to me. "Thanks dude, but I have to go find her and bring her back."

As he typed his response, he spoke it aloud. "What are you going to do? Are you sure I can't come help?"

Nathan's phone buzzed again.

No really thanks man but nobody can help when it comes to Finding Rachel...

THE
JORDAN SPAGNATO
SERIES

Turn the page for an

excerpt from

FINDING
RACHEL

The Jordan Spagnato Series

Book Three

H.J. Harley

My friendship with Jordie was the closest thing I'd ever come to believing that some things were meant to be. For whatever reason...we just clicked. She was one of the only people I could call a 'fugly slut' and she'd respond with something along the lines of, 'That's better than being a dirty ass stank ho'. I knew we'd be friends forever.

Fast forward past a whole lotta fucked up shit, and enter Tyler Duncan, the love of my life, the only man who never ran out on me. Thought, I didn't give him the chance because I bailed first.

Now, Jordie, I knew that bitch would be a little harder to get rid of. She's relentless, even the shit I said to her before I left didn't stop her from searching for me. I'll never forget the look on her face before I walked out her door. I still have to hold my stomach so my insides don't fall out through my ass, because I feel so sick.

"Jordan, I don't see what the problem is? It's not like I exist in your world anymore...except to serve as your bar wench. I'm done, I quit. I quit the bar, I quit Tyler, and I definitely quit you. You're all happy

honkey dory shacked up with your mooooooviiee star husband and your perrrfect life. Why the fuck would you even want me around anymore?" I yelled at Jordie biting back the tears as I balled my fists ready to beat myself over the head with them.

"Rachel, I love you, you're my best...."

"Yeah, yeah, I know, I'm your best friend, right?" I interrupted her. "But that's just it. I'm not any more. He is. Nathan is. Him, your kids, they are everything. And I get it, that's cool I'm fucking ecstatic over the goddamned moon for you...so just let me go without all this bull shit, Jordan." I turned my back to her and faced the door because I couldn't hold back the tears anymore.

"Tyler loves you, Rachel. He's been up for days, looking for you. He hasn't slept, he hasn't eaten, and he hasn't stopped searching the streets for you. He's worried sick and heart broken. He can't even help you because he doesn't know what's wrong. Fuck, I don't even know what's wrong, Rach. Talk to me," she demanded.

With my back still turned to her, I sniffled and stared at the door. "I received another letter in the mail from the Organ Donor place yesterday. It was a letter stating that my father was my match. He wants to reach out to me but since they couldn't give out my information, his case worker mailed it for him." I turned back around to face her even though my face was leaking like a mofo by then.

"And?" Jordie asked me in her 'Just tell me already' tone.

"And? Well, long story short, it turns out he didn't really abandon us and I have a sister. Not a half sister...a full blooded sister." I waited for Jordan to close her mouth and put her eyes back in the sockets as she sat down on the couch. "She told him to go and

to take my three year old sister with him. He wanted to take me, too, but she said no, she was keeping me. He knew why, too...because she knew he'd pay child support for me. I was her meal ticket. As I read it, I didn't believe it of course, until I opened the other letter. It was from my mom telling him I was killed in a bus accident. That he needed to send money for a cremation because I was too badly mangled for an actual open casket funeral and she'd send him some ashes. I was fifteen at the time she wrote it, Jordie. There was also a picture included of him and my sister sitting in the garden they made in my memory. Even had a plaque that said, 'In Memory of a beautiful daughter, sister and soul, our Rachel'. How about that shit?" I said as we both sobbed like two little bitches.

"Rach...if you want to go meet them, I'll go with you. I'll call Nathan and make him come home right now, and I'll pack my shit. You and me, let's go. You can set things straight and maybe have a relationship with them. Then come home and get back to being the old Rachel, because I miss my best friend. I can't stand to see you in so much pain all the time," she pleaded.

I knew she was right. I needed to go see the life I missed out on because my mother was an evil succubus who thrived on other's misery. I also needed to do it alone. After this cluster fuck, it'd only be a matter of time before Tyler bailed on me. Who would blame him? My life went from stable and happy to, 'Houston we have a problem', in four point two seconds.

"How could I marry him if I don't even know who I am anymore?" I said, and adjusted my purse over my shoulder. "You've got what you need Jordan, and it's not me anymore. It was a good run, biotch. I love you,

but I've got to get out of here. Start over."

I walked over to her and we hugged.

"Rachel, please stay. No, fuck that, I won't let you leave. We're sisters. I love you."

Jordie was in a full-blown ugly cry and she hugged me tighter. She wouldn't let me go.

I had to shove her off me. Fuck, what came next would hurt the both of us for a very long time...but I had to, or she would never have let me go. This was worse than breaking up with Tyler...I mean, if I had actually broken it off with Tyler face-to-face, instead of me running off like a fucking coward.

"God dammit, Jordan, why can't you just do one fucking thing that I ask you? You're so effin spoiled it makes me sick. Just forget you ever knew me, you selfish bitch, because after I walk out that door I'm done. You're no longer in my life, in my thoughts, or in my heart. I won't miss you, I won't think about you. I'm finally going to get my life together instead of always putting yours back together," I hissed out at her, turned, and walked out the door.

"Rachel? Rachel? Stop being a space cadet and take this to table eight. *Please*," Kyla said to me as she handed me two Piña Coladas.

"Table eight, coming right up." I rolled my eyes when I turned to walk off.

Bitch. Who the fuck even says 'space cadet' anymore? Kyla Vanderpump, that's who.

Kyla was my floor manager at 'Rain' Night Club at The Palms Casino in Las Vegas. She was nice enough to work under, it's just that I wasn't accustomed to being told what to do. I usually called the shots. A lot had changed in the last two and a half months. I didn't have to think about what I left behind, until they found me. Damn, Nathan and Frank, with their money and mad detective skills. I was hoping to just leave quietly, and Tyler would accept the fact that I got cold feet and wasn't the marrying type.

FINDING RACHEL
available in print and ebook

H.J. grew up in Bricktown New Jersey, a quick train or ferry ride away from New York City. As a teenager and in her early twenties, she loved hanging out in the glamor of NYC. In 2005, she packed up her three cats and moved to California traveling the country until she met her other half in 2005.

After serving twelve years in the Air Force, the man of her dreams ended his military career and they moved to Georgia nearly six years ago. Since then, they've settled down and had their first child. No place has ever come close to replacing the magic of New York City in her mind. When she decided to try her hand at romance novel writing, naturally she set her first book, 'Finding Jordie' there.

H.J. enjoys reading, spending time with her family, really cheesy reality shows, romantic comedies, goofing off, coffee, sunglasses, her furry children and most importantly, being the best Mom possible to her daughter.

CPSIA information can be obtained
at www.ICGtesting.com
Printed in the USA
FFOW04n0756020614
5613FF